D0495086

SWEET DESSERTS

SWEET DESSERTS

LUCY ELLMANN

Published by VIRAGO PRESS Limited
20–23 Mandela Street, Camden Town, London NW1 0HQ

Copyright © Lucy Ellmann 1988

British Library Cataloguing in Publication Data

Ellman, Lucy, *1956—*
Sweet desserts.
I. Title
823′.914[F]

ISBN 0–86068–848–8

Printed in Great Britain by Billings & Sons Ltd, Worcester

FOR MY FATHER.

When sea-turtles manage to meet up,
maybe once a year, they fuck for hours,
shell clacking against shell on the sand.

WANDERLUST

Champaign-Urbana, Illinois 1956

A gray wooden house with diamond window-panes in some places stands amid an endless array of suburban dwellings, each unique in its way but conforming to certain common principles: porches, back-yards, front-yards, attics, basements, buttercups. The sidewalks wind around old oak trees, and there is room between the houses and their foundations for the occasional raccoon to live, and die. It is 92° Fahrenheit.

In the shade of this particular porch, a heavily pregnant woman lies sweating on a swinging seat. A little girl with four dimples on each hand clambers up from the floor to stand beside the woman's belly.

'What's you doing?' she asks.

'I'm trying to sleep,' says her mother. The little girl sits down again, encircled by nonplussed toys, and crosses her legs. Minutes pass, and a few bugs. With a glance towards the prostrate form, the girl gets up and opens the screen door. Her black-and-white saddle shoes negotiate the wooden steps one at a time, and she is warmly embraced by the sun.

All through that summer before her sister's birth, as if she could take a hint, Franny was continually getting lost. She would march in straight lines through neighbors' back-yards, or sneak guiltily through their back-doors. She returned, or was returned, clutching dubious trophies of her wanderings – a toy or cookie of some kind.

In the upstairs bathroom of the big white house across the street, Franny located the medicine cabinet. She dumped all of its pills into the bathtub, to watch the colors collide, and was taken to the hospital to have her empty stomach pumped.

Another time, Franny walked right past a large woman gabbing on the phone and went upstairs to a child's room where she discovered a doll's house that contained elaborate imitation food. Franny propelled all the hors d'oeuvres from one tray into the thick white carpet, and even managed to hide a tiny bucket of watermelon-on-ice in her pocket before being firmly escorted home.

A household on the next block found its collection of dolls' shoes suddenly depleted one day – thirty-six pairs gone – while another family noticed small footprints around their paddling pool and never saw their son's spinning beeno hat again.

Hot, pregnant and shy, Franny's mother trudged down the back alley, hoping that Franny hadn't crossed a street. She asked stunning, sunning women if they'd seen her plumpety child go by, and received cool, blank looks administered from behind dark glasses. Through the combined effects of heat and humiliation, she began to view Franny with some bitterness, and when she awoke one day to the sound of Franny rummaging around in the refrigerator, she decided to lock Franny in her room at nap-time. The two wept in their separate enclaves, absorbing the fact that Franny had become an enemy.

So it was with some dismay that Franny witnessed in mid-October the arrival on this scene of a sibling notable for her placidity. Franny's mother abruptly deserted the battle-ground they'd created together and devoted herself to the stranger, whose curly hair won her Honorable Mention in a baby contest for which Franny hadn't even been entered. Suzy's door was left open at nap-time.

Franny stopped talking. With Suzy satisfyingly ignored in Franny's old baby carriage, the whole family trooped off to consult doctors about Fran's Retarded Speech Development. As a result, her father started reading to her and talking to her more. Fran wet the bed almost every night. Her father told her he too had wet the bed as a child; his mother hung the stained sheets out of his window so the neighbors would know (an old-world cure). Fran sat on his lap, and he confided in this small, wet, troubled person.

The following list refers to recent reports which we hope you have found interesting. How interesting have you found, or do you expect to find, each report?

	Very Interesting	Fairly Interesting	Not so Interesting
Vacuum cleaners	☐	☐	☐
Low-fat food	☐	☐	☐
Dishwashers	☐	☐	☐
Toasters	☐	☐	☐

THE HEART OPERATION

Suzy was a sickly child (in whom the family doctor eventually noticed an operable heart defect), a quality which endeared her to her mother while further alienating Fran. Suzy had to rest on the short trip to the grocery store: first, she would start to drop behind, then she would have to sit down on the curb, panting. She rode in her stroller as long as she could still fit into it.

She also rode a tricycle until peer-group pressure (Fran's scorn) forced her to abandon it. Suzy learned to ride a bike at lunch-time every day for two weeks, when no other children were outdoors. When her efforts landed her in a rose-bush, her mother plucked the thorns from her thigh.

Where physical stamina wasn't involved, Suzy proved to be extremely conservative. She held tentative WASPish prejudices common in the neighborhood, such as her deep ignorance of the working class and other races (did they too love?). She envied TV children their gentile names, toys, foods, their inevitable glasses of milk and geometrical hunks of chocolate cake after school. Melissa from two doors down was in this mould: not only did her mother sport the most perpetual tan on the block, but her father was in advertizing. Melissa always had a sample of whatever toy or soft drink he was currently popularizing.

It was Melissa who explained politics to Suzy early on: the Republicans like trees and animals and the countryside, the Democrats like cities and factories and pollution. Melissa

4

was a Republican, and a Presbyterian – both unusually long words in her vocabulary. Inspired by her, though without Melissa's knowledge, Suzy stole a silver St Christopher pendant from Melissa's sister's jewelry-box, and thus equipped, pursued a phase of clandestine Christian fervor. She prayed in bed every night that the Lord should take her soul if she died before she awoke (an odd bargain, she always thought). But Fran managed to find the weak spot in Suzy's piety. When Fran yelled once, 'Goddam you, Suzy!', Suzy replied in kind and promptly excommunicated herself.

The Schwarz family's only official Sunday ritual was making pancakes. They followed Irma Rombauer's instructions, except that Fran and Suzy always fought over who got to make the well in the sifted ingredients. Their father poured the egg mixture into this well (he called eggs 'aigues' for some reason). Then Fran and/or Suzy stirred it up, neverminding the lumps. Suzy's only complaint on Sundays was that the orange juice had lumps in it too, being freshly squeezed.

Suzy liked to be bored by TV shows, first by Mr Green Jeans and Captain Kangaroo in the morning before school, and then by Bozo the Clown when she came home for lunch. The lunch itself left something to be desired. They always had Chicken Noodle Soup (Fran's favorite) and Tuna Fish sandwiches (ditto). Suzy would have preferred more Kool-Aid, or Hawaiian Punch, and peanut-butter-and-jelly sandwiches. But she didn't care what other children got after ice-skating – she and Fran always had hot chocolate with marshmallows floating on top, while *Samson et Dalila* crackled on the record-player.

Dalila: *Réponds, réponds à ma tendresse!*
Verse-moi, verse-moi l'ivresse!
Samson: *Dalila! Dalila! je t'aime!*

At such times, Suzy would refrain from asking her mother to put on Petula Clark singing 'Downtown', and concentrate instead on the melting process taking place in her marshmallows.

> The mixture should be of medium stiff consistency, and flavoured with lemon. Pipe out on wafer paper oval shapes, dust over with sugar, make an impression down centre and bake.

Fran taught Suzy how to balance a book on her head, masturbate, scramble eggs, and bite her toenails. She despised Suzy's choice in friends, and despised her for tagging along with hers, but usually let her in the end. Suzy in turn was secretly protective of Fran, passionately resenting all ill treatment of her older sister. But Fran was the most noble: when Suzy spent her eighth Halloween in the hospital having the hole in her heart repaired, Fran collected an extra bag of candy for her, explaining the sorrowful situation at every doorway, and didn't eat Suzy's even when she'd finished her own.

Fran was good at reading, while Suzy fell behind and had to be coached by her father on Saturday afternoons, tears blurring one Aesop's fable after another – 'Hard work brings prosperity.' Fran had a guinea pig, Suzy had mice: she had to have more than one, since guinea pigs are bigger than mice. Many of Fran's clothes were red; an equivalent number of Suzy's were blue, their mother's favorite color.

Fran always won their arguments, by physical force if necessary, unless Suzy tattle-taled, a habit Fran despised. Fran also decided on their activities, which included picnics, bike-hikes, and dramatizations of their dreams. They formed a secretive anarchistic organization called the T.N.T. Club with Melissa, and published a neighborhood newspaper at least twice.

They memorized subversive poetry:

> Boodleheimer, boodleheimer,
>   CLAP, CLAP, CLAP!
> Boodleheimer, boodleheimer,
>   CLAP, CLAP, CLAP!
> The more you boodle, the less you heimer.
> The more you heimer, the less you boodle.
> Boodleheimer, boodleheimer,
>   CLAP, CLAP, CLAP!

When they wrote a book together about a practical, well-behaved sister, and a flamboyant, extravagant one, Fran wanted to draw all the pictures of the dull specimen, having observed one for so long. Suzy was supposed to draw the fun one. Likewise, the dull sister's possessions, and the fun one's.

> Gwendoline is an impractical child. An impractical child is a child who does not always choose the best thing for his or her health. Sometimes the thing he or she does is silly or not good and sometimes the results are expensive. But sometimes as you will find out in this book, the impractical child does the right thing.

> Gertrude is a practical child. She usually tries to be good and inexpensive. She tries to do the right thing for her health, minds her manners and tries not to be silly. She wears plain clothes and does not dress up as fancily as Gwendoline. But sometimes, as you will find out in this book, Gertrude does the wrong thing.

They sent *Gwendoline and Gertrude* to a publisher who returned it with a note that Fran found offensive and Suzy considered reasonable.

One day when they were all sitting on the front porch, Fran and a friend of hers asked Suzy how babies are made – they said they wanted to make sure she had it right. Suzy knew by now that the version offered by Melissa's mother, that babies are conceived somehow while the parents are asleep, wouldn't do, but she remained somewhat hazy on the subject.

'The man puts his penis in the woman's vagina,' she ventured, immediately embarrassed by her own choice of latinate words.

'Yeah, and then what?'

'Well, then, then he pees in her?'

Fran and Co. laughed and laughed, but didn't suggest any alternative.

PROBLEM: Fran's Chinese spoon, red flowers winding all along its stem, sits broken in a kitchen drawer for over a year.

Suzy finds it, glues it together, and calls it hers.

Fran reclaims it and eats Chicken Noodle Soup with it.

QUESTION: Whose spoon is it?

Dear Mommy,
I am running
away. I hope
you don't mind
me taking a   *P.S. Please*
sandwich.   *take care*
love, Suzy   *of my mice.*

Fran found her four blocks away, holding her weekend bag with its pyjamas and sandwich, wondering where to go, since she had already reached the boundary of her usual zone.

FRAN

Bone two large eels, fill them with diced truffles.
Wrap in a piece of muslin and tie with string. Cook
in wine and well-flavoured fish stock. Drain,
unwrap, and cool under a press.

Wivenhoe, Essex, England   1983

'Why am I wasting my time with this person?' thought Fran,
as she surveyed the floral arrangement Rod had made of the
beer coasters around the central tin ashtray. He was presenting
his entranced look and recounting once again his experience
of seeing a bear in the Rocky Mountains one Christmas day.
His eyes focused momentarily on obscure corners of the
room.

'Christmas morning! and there I was, after a night holed
up in the snow, just crawling onto my feet when suddenly,
out of nowhere, or so it seemed –'

'Came a bear,' assisted Fran.

'Yeah!' Pause for an attractive bout of wistful eye-
sparkling.

'You want another drink?' asked Fran.

'Oh sure, hon.'

Apart from the pressing fact that the guy resembled a
Greek – or at least an American – god, with his brown locks,

9

reddish stubble, and hamburger-fed flesh, what the hell was she doing with Rod McMead? Fran got up before he could start another sentence, and went to order the drinks, distracting herself with thoughts of peanuts and sex. The peanuts they shared out immediately. These stirred in Rod a memory of the trip he'd taken with his ex-wife to the Pyramids, where they'd eaten honeyed peanut pastries, ridden on camels, and avoided lettuce. This in turn led him on to fishing in the Lake District, a story Fran hadn't actually heard before, but she didn't encourage him to tell it: she felt a need to conserve fresh data for the sake of future evenings.

At last, the requisite drinks and anecdotes swallowed, they headed back to Fran's flat, with its unusually full-sized fridge, its defunct greenhouse, and its lack of Central Heating. Fran threw two new brown envelopes onto the window-sill with all the other unopened business mail, and Rod began his exercise regime: fifty push-ups, fifty sit-ups, twenty-five wall-jumps. Wall-jumps were supposedly good for the bad back which periodically laid Rod flat (a mysterious injury dating from the time of his first marriage). Late at night, in pleasanter weather, Rod liked to run very fast up and down the hill outside, imagining a confirmatory trail of steam following him as he sped this way and that.

After his work-out, Rod poked his head around her bedroom door, in order to display the enticing juxtaposition of his glittering muscles and his nonchalance – before tripping off to have a bath. Fran had once been impressed by all this.

Reluctant to be so thoroughly on show herself, she was in bed by the time he returned, soil-free. Then, craving the final physical challenge of the day, Rod plopped down on top of her, crushing her ribs in the now familiar way. He then pursued his method of fucking which involved no foot or eye contact (for different impenetrable reasons). As she fingered the perfectly indented buttocks, Fran once again acknowledged that he was a great catch.

What thing do you think Gwendoline likes best
and what thing do you think Gertrude likes best?

What thing do *you* like best?

She struggled out from under a heavy arm at 5.58, by Rod's
watch, which had glowed in her face all night. She made
strong coffee in her espresso machine, cappucinoed some
milk with the somewhat intimidating milk-steamer Suzy had
giver her, dolloped morello cherry jam and Philadelphia
Cream Cheese on a toasted blueberry muffin, and had breakfast in the dining section of her living-room. She added this
plate and cup to the accumulated chaos in the sink, went to
the bathroom, threw up, brushed her teeth, washed her hair,
and fuddled around looking for something to wear.

Guy goes to the doctor.
  'Doc, you gotta help me. I ain't feelin' so good.'
  The doctor examines him but doesn't find anything
obviously wrong, so he says, 'Suppose you tell me exactly
what you do, from the minute you get up in the morning to
when you go to bed at night.'
  'Sure thing, doc. Well, let's see. I get outa bed, put on
some slippers, go into the bathroom, have a pee, throw up,
wash my face, brush my –'
  'Wait a minute there! Could you just repeat that for me
please?'
  'Okay. Well, I get up, I get my slippers on, I go have a pee,
I throw up, I –'
  'You throw up?! Every morning?!'
  'Sure. Doesn't everybody?'

Fran had more coffee with Rod later, as she watched him
shave his big American jaw. His inane self-confidence thrilled
her in the mornings. She imagined him standing beside a big
hot car on a sunset strip, the predominant colors purple and

tan with a dash of bright yellow. A HoJo, or maybe a jojoba, in the background. And a bee-hived blonde or red-head just visible behind the windscreen.

He always left for work early: with or without back trouble, Rod had an American's attitude to the rigors of academic life. He'd taught classes at 8.00 a.m. in Texas. And at Essex, he'd once lectured from a stretcher on Piranesi. His students, initially delighted, soon collapsed with him into a torpor which was not dispelled by the slides of dizzying prison chambers Rod had selected.

Fran wasn't going into the university that day. She had to work on an article about signs of violence in art, for *D.K. Magazine* (short for 'Deliberate Kaprice'). She got down to it as soon as Rod had left, typing fast. Once engrossed, Fran was in another world, full of a sense of her own power. She wanted her readers to have to hold on to their seats, and their hats. She began by quoting *King Lear* at them:

> 'She that will sliver and disbranch from her
> material sap, perforce must wither
> And come to deadly use.'

What we are witnessing in the Twentieth Century is a full-scale adolescent rebellion among artists, who self-consciously abuse their *mater*-ials in order to aid their own creativity. The rough handling of paint, in such artists as Chardin and Manet, has developed into a ruffian's art which is deliberately destined to disintegrate – the 'I-don't-fit-in' syndrome, expressed through paint that doesn't stick on.

At about 12.00, Fran turned off her typewriter, her desk-lamp and her gas-fire, and went to the kitchen to make herself a nice lunch of Tuna Fish au Gratin (open sandwich with toasted cheese on top, with which Fran had first become acquainted in her Junior High School Home Economics class). She consumed it along with a big glass of orange juice while reading Anaïs Nin's erotica, but only the warm tuna gave her any sense of well-being. After throwing up, she turned her typewriter, her desk-lamp and her gas-fire back on.

Fundamental Facts about Food
*How to Eat for Health, Strength
and Efficiency*

1. Make either breakfast or the noon-meal the hearty meal of the day. Avoid heavy meals at night.

2. Take care to chew each morsel thoroughly. This greatly aids digestion and bowel action.

3. Drink four to six pints of water daily.

Rod called at 2.30 to find out what time they were going to meet at the pub that night. After she hung up, Fran began to feel a bit flustered. She went to have a look at herself in the full-length mirror in the hall. She squeezed herself into her tightest pair of jeans, by lying on her back on the floor and squirming around. Once they were zipped up, she took another look in the mirror. She took the jeans off and put on a track-suit.

It was cold outside, not a hint of sun, as she embarked on her run through Wivenhoe. She passed some little boys at the end of her road who jeered unintelligibly at her. Near the train station, a man said 'Cor!' in response to Fran's bouncing breasts, and a little further on, a drunk moved out of a passageway in order to say, 'Smile, Love. Can't be that bad.' Fran had to swerve to avoid touching him.

When she got home, she removed a rock-hard blueberry muffin from the freezer, wrestled the two halves apart, toasted, buttered and ate them. She tried to vomit afterwards but couldn't, so let it pass.

> 10. Secure three free bowel movements
> daily by the abundant use of fruits,
> Sanitarium Cooked Bran, greens and
> other laxative foods, such as Fig-Bran,
> Branola, Vita-Bits, Fig Marmalade, Laxa,
> Colax, Lacto-Dextrin, Psylla, Paraffin
> Oil, Paralax or Paramels.

She had a bath, shampooed her hair again, shaved in deference to Rod's American predilections, and put on make-up, Gentle Support tights, and a dark red velvet dress with a low décolletage. Around it she buckled a belt of gold chain. She slotted heavy golden globs into her newly punctured ear-lobes with some difficulty, and fastened a choker Rod had given her around her neck. It chinked against the earrings and rubbed against her collarbone every time she moved her head. She added a thick brassy bracelet to the general effect, and then paused to admire the twenty-seven clearly distinguishable bones in her hand. Would Rod find her sexy for another day?

> The dissonance, or discrepancy, between the way a
> medium has been used, and the overall effect of the
> work of art, is particularly glaring in illusionist art,
> where the material is forced to malign itself by
> looking like something it is not. The paint is made
> subordinate to a veneer it has itself created, and we
> become, like Pygmalion, dazzled by fantasy and
> unaware of the stone.

> *'Réponds, réponds à ma tendresse!'*

OUT WENT THE CANDLE, AND WE WERE LEFT DARKLING

Basic principles of automatic latches – Speed and feed control – Four jaw and angle-plate chucking – Sectional views – Half views – Special attachments – Testing stresses in material – Temporary repair and salvage – Holding devices – Making split bearings – Piston troubles – Self-acting lathes.

Champaign-Urbana   1969

Fran's parents were determined to help her with her weight problem. First, they took her to a psychiatrist who told Fran her father was trying to starve her. So then they took her to a dietitian who sent them home with a week's menu. They were supposed to give her minute-steak for breakfast. Suzy wanted to have minute-steak for breakfast too, and soon the whole family was eating minute-steak for breakfast, none of them getting any thinner.

Fran began to eat non-protein in private, in the form of crumb-cakes. Suzy ate chocolate brownies on the way home from school. When she became allergic to nuts, she ate non-

15

nutty brownies, and when she became allergic to chocolate, she switched to crumb-cakes.

Their father was writing the first of his many scathing attacks on Rubens who, up until then, had enjoyed quite a high reputation at the University of Illinois.

> '. . . His famous eroticism has, with changes in male taste, begun to seem increasingly eccentric. The inevitable expanses of slithering, indecipherable flesh, like a body turned inside out and stretched into infinity, tire the eye, and appal the mind. What *can* these women have been eating?'

All that summer, Suzy and her mother sat on the porch eating peaches in cream for breakfast. Blueberries, sometimes. Fran was at music camp: she was particularly good at double-tonguing.

Fran struggled to get her violet knickerbockers on fast, before the other girls came back from swimming. How she hated swimming en masse – like ducks scrambling around for bread. The new thing today was to call Fran a commie because she'd declared her dissatisfaction with Nixon and the Viet Nam War. Fran grabbed her flute and got out of the cabin just in time. She walked under big pine trees, thinking how awful she looked in violet knickerbockers and Tyrolean suspenders and thick white socks and white blouses and baggy sweaters, in fact the whole stupid outfit that some sadist had considered appropriate for Michigan summers at some point for some reason. She arrived late for the mass flute class, and was treated to the standard public humiliation by the maestro. Afterwards, she went to the Lodge for a milk-shake and french fries. She spoke to no one. All the other girls were more beautiful, more Jewish, more popular. Some even had boyfriends in the Boys' Section.

16

33. Avoid condiments – mustard, pepper, pepper-sauce, cayenne, vinegar, pickles – all the irritating spices and condiments.

Suzy's One Year Diary

Franny gives Mommy an unhappy birthday. She probably hardly realized. Franny isn't always so nice to us anymore. She probably thinks we're all a bunch of queer balls, though I think *she's* the queer ball.

Today we went to Chicago. I bought a new culottes skirt, Franny bought a new suit, and Mommy bought a cute purple dress. At first I didn't think it was fair that they got things with tops and I didn't, but when we went to another store, Daddy bought me switchable sun-glasses, and that evened it all out.

Today we rehearsed the love scene. Scott sat down next to me, our legs touching, put his warm hands on my shoulder and we sat there, cheek to cheek. We practiced this a no. of times. I think I like him and he likes me.

Yesterday I lied to Melanie and told her that Scott really kissed me but he didn't. This morning she went and told Scott that he had kissed me and maybe that I had told her so. If Scott ever did like me, he probably doesn't now, and if he didn't he probably never will, thanks to Dear Sweet Melanie.

Melanie and I went downtown to buy some sandals. We went to Arrnolds shoe store and found some nice sandals. They were too small in all the sizes the man brought. So I picked out a different kind I liked. After getting me some of those in another size, he went off to help another lady. We sat there about ten mins. waiting for him to come back, but he didn't, so after slapping my knees and impatiently sighing 'God!' (and after we'd gotten everybody's attention) we walked out. HA! HA!

My 13th birthday. I started to menstruate. I told Mommy but told her not to tell Daddy. We had to tell Franny, so I could borrow some Kotex. Then we went downtown and bought pant suits. Mommy gave us the charge plate. For presents I got: 1 pant suit (from Mommy)
           1 skirt suit (from Mommy)
           1 blue shirt with stripes (from Mommy)
           1 box Russell Stover candy (from Mommy)
           1 pack personalized pencils (from Franny)
I decorated my cake. This was the best birthday I've ever had.

9.30 AM: I'm at school. Franny is taking day off. Mommy is in kitchen. Daddy in bathroom, occupied with morning defacation.
    Mommy faints. Comes to. Vomits blood. Calls for Daddy. Franny hears. Franny calls for Daddy. Daddy hears. Comes downstairs. Calls hospital. Mommy says: 'I think it's a cerebral hemerage. Tell them to be careful with my head.' Ambulance comes. They speed towards hospital.
    4.00 PM: I arrive home. Note says 'Suzy, Mommy and Daddy are at hosp. having tests.' I think it's just more thyroid tests – nothing serious.

Franny comes home and tells me what happened. I cry a lot because I think it's cancer, and she will die. I cry a lot. I can't stop. I run and throw away all cigs in sight.

4.05: Ruth Pevner picks Franny and I up. We go to hosp.

At hospital – we walk into small room – put on white gowns and large plastic boots. We walk through the door. The third bed on the right: there lay Mommy. One eye covered by a gauze pad, the other eye uncovered. It did not open and was all red. A white bandage covered her head. I noticed they must have had to shave her hair. Beside her was the introveinous thing and the cardiagram machine. We stayed 10 mins. Then we spend evening with Ruth. We have for desert choc. Mousse. It's abonabable.

There was once a gray house in which hot chocolate was drunk with marshmallows floating on the top. The kitchen drawers contained a haphazard collection of inherited silver souvenir spoons. Tasteful Niagara Falls ones from some honeymoon. A Chicago World's Fair (1883-1933) spoon, with air-planes, domed buildings and the latest developments in bridge-engineering encrusted on its bowl. There was a whole set of president-spoons, commemorating a variety of achievements: Morse telegrams for Tyler (10th), and a horribly bumpy Berlin airlift for Truman, no good for anything except stirring. There was also a crowd of grapefruit spoons, with sharp-toothed edges: Daddy never passed a grapefruit spoon without buying it.

After another Neurological Event, my mother died. When Daddy told me, we stood there in the kitchen for a moment, and then clutched each other in sudden unexpected communion and sobbed the same strange sobs.

Mommy was buried in one of those cemeteries that has tiny plaques in the ground to make it easer to mow the grass.

No artificial flavorings or preservatives.

Various interpretations of the maternal role were offered us: some people brought lasagna, others took Franny and me on long drives to glimpse blindingly white, be-columned mansions built in the Colonial style.

Protose
A vegetable meat. One of the most
interesting discoveries of modern times.
Looks like meat, tastes like meat, smells
like meat, has the composition of meat,
and even the fibre of meat. May be
cooked in all the different ways in which
meat is ordinarily prepared – boiled,
stewed, roasted, or broiled, or may be
eaten cold, direct from the can.

A nun with a crush on our father moved in to await his infrequent returns. She told us what to eat, what to wear, when to do our homework and when to go to bed, taught us how to peel tomatoes, and told us we were lucky to have mirrors to discover our pimples *in*.

Trim the lozenge shapes and blanch in
boiling water.

I took to reading the phone-book in my mother's study, and acquired an endless supply of Kotex sanitary pads, transported home precariously on the handlebars of my bicycle – they were selling cheap.

Television adverts do not seem to care for people's feelings anymore. When I and my two daughters were watching during a commercial break, to my horror an advertisement for sanitary towels was shown. Whatever next? Please take this off.

UNDER SATISFACTORY ENDOTRACHEAL ANAESTHESIA, AFTER THE USUAL PREPARATION AND DRAPING, THE MEDIASTINUM WAS ENTERED THROUGH A STERNAL SPLITTING INCISION. THE PERICARDIAL SAC WAS OPENED WIDELY, THE HEART WAS EXAMINED.

SUZY

KISS SOMEONE YOU LOVE WHEN YOU GET THIS AND MAKE MAGIC

This letter has been sent to you for GOOD LUCK. The original copy is in New England. It has been around the world nine times. You will receive Good Luck within four days of receiving this letter providing you in turn send it out through the mail. This is no joke.

Please send 20 copies to people you think need Good Luck. Do not send money as faith has no price. Do not keep this letter. It must leave your hands within 96 hours. An officer received 70,000.00. Joe Elliott received 40,000.00 and lost it because he broke the chain. While in the Philippines, Gene Welch lost his wife within six days after reading this letter because he failed to circulate it. However, before her death he received 7,775.00.

North London   1983

Confronted by so many naked behinds, each different, some perfect in their way, but most wavering in the balance, I considered the purpose of posteriors. They're something to sit on, it's true, but people with minimal buttocks do manage. Are they there merely to protect assholes? I decided their job was to blur social boundaries by looking equally incongruous on everybody. As I ducked into a dingy cubicle, I awarded the same function to feet. Ditto, ears, noses, and hair distributions. Big toes. Little toes!

I shoved myself into my blue-and-yellow-striped bathing-suit, with its misguided air of good cheer. After trying several arrangements of my breasts, I settled for the one involving maximum, if temporary, uplift. As I plodded out to the pool I became more and more conscious of my jiggling dimpled thighs. Feeling the solace of my irreverence towards the anatomy of othes recede somewhat, I delivered myself gratefully into the chlorinated camouflage.

A dark wet head bobbed nearby: a man was watching me. I hung on to most of my self-consciousness in his honor. When he was still observing me a width or two of the pool later, I began to tackle the remote possibility of being fancied more or less in my birthday suit. Must be a jerk. I swam some more, got red in the face, and checked my admirer again. He was still clinging to the side of the pool, immovable as a limpet, but now looking at someone else. I paddled on, relieved.

Back in the changing-room, I read through all the heart shapes adorning the walls of my cubicle. There it was made clear that Julie loved Colin T. OK, that Sharon & Donna & Patsy had formed some sort of liaison, that Pussy 4 Cocky, and that in fact love, like bottoms, is common to all.

> INNOCENCE! One hour of GENUINE
> housewives, young and mature ladies
> with big tits. Never seen before.

I'd bought *Colossus* for its personal ads, which it claimed were Britain's best, but they offered only frantic SM, thorough CP, stunning TV, unbearably ET (Erotic or Exquisite Torment), and enemas. Hardly worth buying the mag, which had been something of an Ordeal in itself. I'd managed it by assembling a pile of varied publications in front of the newsagent, along with a pint of milk and a packet of digestive biscuits. My guilt about the cookies somehow alleviated my shame about buying soft porn, and I was doing fine, I felt, until someone behind me called out for penis tissues.

Unphased, the cashier said, 'Kleenex? Over there.'

I hurried out with my shady purchases, trying to look deadpan.

> HUGE SUE (84-70-73), for lovers of
> enormous ladies and well-filled knickers.

Where did she find Size 73 knickers, I wondered smugly to myself as I sat in my Morris Minor (four-door, unreliable in cold weather, naked prancing women painted by me along dashboard), munching digestive biscuits. Did all the ads for fat women reflect a hitherto imperceptible erotic trend, or just mass unemployment among sexually-inclined obese people? I turned to the fussier type of personal ad:

> ARE YOU OUT THERE? Ex-Company
> Director (75) seeks full-bosomed lady-
> friend (26-56) to share the gardening.
> Good sense of humour a help.

> Reasonable-looking female, 37, emotion-
> ally vulnerable but essentially positive.
> Seeks sensitive, non-smoking male.
> Quick.

> MALE, average build, likes TV. Seeks
> female soul-mate.

> ME: Non-scene, blond, fit, attractive.
> YOU: Same.

> Give A Girl A Chance! Lively vivacious
> plump career-girl, young 49 and solvent.
> Passion for all good things. Now
> looking for that genuine sincere some-
> body who's into long-term hetero
> commitments, O.N.O. Long letter
> please. A.L.A.

> BIG RICH SONUVABITCH wants
> HAREM of tall slim MODEL types
> (16-22) for HIGH JINKS on YACHT in
> CARIBBEAN. Recent photo and birth
> certificate.

> PRETTY sporty girl wants KINKY
> guy. Anyone for tattoos?

I was beginning to feel a little dispirited by this remorselessly
motivated crowd, each at a peak of purposefulness, resolved
to avoid fatties, shelve the problems of a lifetime and go
dating. The few that seemed at all possible admitted in the
end to a taste for wind-surfing or D. H. Lawrence – dreadful
to have to mooch around in a bathing-suit all day waiting for
a fuck. I nestled deeper into my Morris Minor (which Jeremy
had likened to a bath-tub) and chomped cookies. I was
thinking up my own ad:

> FAT damsel-in-distress, own car, hair,
> teeth, breasts, seeks extracurricular SEX
> with a Prince Charming, or Semi-
> Charming, to keep the wolf at bay.

I twirled the cookie-packet in the air to reseal it, stuffed it
into the glove compartment behind old AA maps (a careful
eater), and drove to the laundromat. There, stared at by the
concave lenses of numerous washing-machines, sat two

women discussing world affairs. One was sorting through piles of service washes while the other, a laundromat hanger-on, concentrated on finding new subjects to fret about.

Two young men came in to fetch their meagre, well-cooked wardrobes from the dryers. (Why do men go to laundromats with so few clothes? I wait till there are at least two rubbish-bags full.) The inactive woman asked them about someone called Maggie, so I assumed they all knew each other, but it turned out to be the opener for an inconclusive line of complaint against the Prime Minister. When the men had left, she instantly moved on to the subject of Men.

'Can you believe staying with a man after he beat you up?!' she asked her companion.

'I don't care,' said the other woman, lifting a huge blue plastic basket of washing. 'Even if I had a baby coming, I'd leave him.' So saying, she marched into an ante-room. The other woman began to eye me in her absence.

'Terrible! Always out for themselves! And only after one thing.'

I mustered a polite smile.

'*You* ever been married, darling?'

'No.'

'Keep it that way. You American?'

'Yeah.'(You can't keep that hidden for long.)

'What do you think of that guy?'

'Who?'

'That Reagan.'

'Oh. I hate him.'

'Just as bad as her, what's her name?'

'Thatcher?'

'Yeah,' she said, and then paused. 'No good with children.'

'Who?'

'Men!'

Turtles have been toothless for more
than 150,000,000 years.

THE POCKET GOPHER, of the
Mississippi Basin, has soft brown fur
and is very mole-like in his life and
habits.

I drove up Finchley Road, turned off on Parsifal, drove along
Agamemnon Ave, Clytemnestra Terrace and Ajax Road, and
turned right on Leda. Suddenly aware of an upsurge of
resentment – a dim sense that my present vehicular direction-
lessness did not tally with the fact that I had paid most of our
rent for the past few months – I turned off Fortune Green,
and with the customary feeling of abdominal constriction ('a
shudder in the loins . . .'), parked on Ulysses Road: I was
home. As I applied my ill-fitting key to the front door, I
could already hear Irving conducting one of his loud,
meandering telephone conversations in the hallway.
    'Oh yes, can't complain. What? I said, MUSTN'T
GRUMBLE. Yes. What about you? You are? The window-
cleaner came today. Tramp, tramp, tramp through my
kitchen. WINDOW-CLEANER: TRAMP, TRAMP,
TRAMP. What? Oh, to get water, I suppose. There was a
good programme on telly today, about Jersey. JERSEY.
Yes. Oh, all right then, Leo. Some good TV tonight. Talk to
you next week then. All right. All right then, bye.'
    I managed to clamber into the house and up the stairs with
my two rubbish-bags full of washing and two carrier-bags
full of shopping before Irving could hang up, thus sparing
myself a similar tête-à-tête, and no doubt disappointing Irving.
After dragging the bags to their respective destinations, I
knocked on the door of the front room. Jeremy was sitting in
an armchair with a dictionary by his side, directing his every

neutrino towards the completion of *The Times* crossword. Little circles of anagram letters embellished the bottom margin. He looked up briefly.

'I'm back,' I informed him.

'So I see,' said he.

'Do you want a cup of coffee?' I asked.

'Ooh, yes please.' He took my hand briefly to betoken gratitude, and then resumed his concentration on the puzzle in his lap.

After making tea for myself and coffee for Jeremy, I unloaded all the shopping. One of my chief pleasures in life was dealing with store-bought food – all so virginally packaged yet bursting to be opened. I lined up a regiment of Jeremy's favorite yoghurts, on the only shelf in the £7 fridge I'd bought at a Hampstead garage sale: its previous owners were heading for an even higher altitude (perhaps Muswell Hill). I snapped up a few of their least snazzy possessions.

I peeled open the one yoghurt I'd bought for myself, and tried it with my finger. Champagne Rhubarb. To go with my yoghurt and my tea, I located the long stiff phallus of Fig Bars and extracted two, or maybe three. I hid these behind my yoghurt while I delicately re-aligned the plastic shrink-wrap around the remaining Fig Bars, sealed the wound with the Supa-Dupa Glue I'd just bought for this purpose, and placed the deceptive packet on the top shelf along with the other biscuits and crisps I'd gotten for Jeremy (whose skinni-ness is one of the miracles of this world). I felt pretty confident that he was unlikely to interfere with the Fig Bars, as long as I kept him well supplied with cheese balls.

49. Eat only natural foods. Avoid flesh meats of all sorts as these are unnatural foods. Use Protose, Nuttolene and nuts instead.

The stink of Supa-Dupa Glue filled the kitchen as I started on the supper. Still timid of inner organs, I overcooked the Chicken Livers with Guinness and Bacon and Onions that Jeremy had taught me to make. I called him to supper. He didn't hear me. I went to get him. He had just lit a cigarette. He started to shuffle books and papers around, and gathered coffee cups into intimate groups. He drew my attention to a mildly amusing article in *The Times*. Having first apologized for the fact that it was early Schoenberg, he turned off the record-player, and then the gas-fire. He went to the loo. From there, he proceeded to the bathroom, where he scrubbed his fingernails and squirted contact lens solution on each contact lens before re-inserting it.

When he reached the dining-room, he looked at his plate of over-cooked Chicken Livers with Guinness and Bacon and Onions, and went out again. Returning with a glass of water, he picked up the plate and said, 'Do you mind if I watch the Cricket Highlights?'

By the time it had occurred to me to say, 'I thought you didn't like cricket highlights,' he had reached the bedroom. There, he turned on the light, pulled the curtains, lit the gas-fire, switched on the TV, shut the door, took off his shoes, lay down on the bed, and lit a cigarette. I was relieved he'd gone – food tended to stick in my throat when he was around. I ate as fast as I could, just in case the highlights were too chiaroscuro for him.

'I have been a victim of constipation
for thirty years. Recently I became
acquainted with Battle Creek products
and began using them as per instructions
from the demonstrator. I have used the
Complete Battle Creek Diet System,
using Bran, Agar, Paramels or Mineral
Oil, and Battle Creek cereal foods with

liberal doses of Lacto-Dextrin, Meltose,
and Fig Bromose. Now I have two or
three thorough eliminations every day
and feel much encouraged.'

The gentleman is one of the greatest
producers of movie films in the world
and his duties are most exacting. His
enthusiasm for biologic living is
unbounded.

I pumiced my feet with some ferocity in the bathtub and
headed for bed. The room was very hot, and Jeremy was
asleep. When I sat down on the bed, he got up groggily,
turned off the TV, said, 'Must get on, pull my finger out [an
expression he knew I disliked, for its connotations of sexual
withdrawal],' and left the room. I put his half-eaten supper
outside the door, turned the gas-fire off and the TV back on,
and got into bed. There was a black-and-white movie just
starting, about three wives who each receive a letter from the
same friend saying she's running off with one of their
husbands that day, but no one knows which husband has
been selected. Each woman's marriage is then investigated
for flaws. I fell asleep before finding out which marriage
deserved perpetuation, or which husband skidaddled – if any.

REASON NOT THE NEED

Why the Blues?
A book for neurasthenics, nervous
dyspeptics, bilious, despondent folks. Shows
them the way out of their miseries. Easy to
read, practical, interesting. Illustrated 339
pages. Price $2.25

Champaign-Urbana   1970

When I had perused a good quarter of my mother's telephone
directory, Franny decided that what I needed was a new love
interest. We were sitting in the kitchen when the nun was out
and a casserole-bearing neighbor had just left.

'You know Kate has a brother at school in Eighth Grade?'
Franny asked me. Kate was her best friend.

'What does he look like?' I asked.

'Long red hair and glasses.'

'Oh, yeah, I know him.'

'What do you think of him?'

'I think he's a really beautiful boy. Why?'

'He told Kate he thinks you're pretty.'

From then on, Franny and Kate worked hard on getting
me and Chris together: Franny told Kate I liked him and Kate
told Chris. She told him to talk to me, but instead we were
careful to avoid each other. The next weekend, I was leafing

31

through the phone-book when the telephone rang. Franny ran into the room and picked it up. After a short, muffled conversation, she hung up and said, 'Suzy, Chris is coming over.'

I rushed around, brushing my teeth and putting ribbons in my hair. By the time I got out of the bathroom, Kate and Chris had arrived. They were all standing in Mommy's study. I walked in as casually as I could. Franny and Kate instantly departed for Franny's room.

'How are you?' I asked Chris.

'Fine. How are you?' he answered.

'Fine. Do you have Mrs C. for Math?' (I was pretty sure that he did.)

'No.'

'You're lucky.'

Kate came back in and asked us if we'd like to go on a bike-hike with them.

'Do you want to go?' Chris asked me.

'I guess so,' I replied.

> SWM, principled, open, liberal, politically as well as physically sound, distinguished bearing, cultured, articulate, literate, extensively traveled, compassionate, tender, attuned. Into self-hypnosis, mysticism, Tai Chi, I Ching, the Cabbala, extra-terrestrial life-forms, reincarnation, Yin/Yang, the whole shebang. Well-turned-out, clean-cut, highly presentable, in fact a successful human being to the extent that self-actualization is ever completed. Own secluded sun-filled garden, gracious home. Ballroom dancer. SEEKS attractive, thrifty, loving lady, not over 20 lbs. overweight, with mind, job, and apartment of her own, strong sense of her own identity, autonomy, and self-sufficiency, and a serious commitment to own work and hobbies.

Together in oneness to embark on actualizing the infinite potential, mystery, romance, awe, and poignant sweetness of life awaiting those who dare to reach for their shooting star. Come be my love and let us soar. Libbers, grouchers, whiners, and those who have all the answers, no. Photo.

I threw myself into my love affair with Chris. We would meet after school and walk around holding hands and periodically passionately embracing for tight-lipped kisses (we'd tried French kissing but decided against it). Despite all of Franny's world-weary advice that I should play hard-to-get, I found myself quite incapable of working up convincing feminine wiles. Instead I told Chris that when I saw him coming up the hill from the Gym, I felt like I was melting. He was a bit embarrassed – too corny. But when I told him I loved him, he echoed the sentiment, as was proper.

He lay on top of me in Franny's room once, where we had gone to listen to Laura Nyro records. Another time, we found a tiny chapel stuck on the end of a church near Melanie's house. We sat in there cooling off, and then Chris felt my breasts for the first time. Daddy discovered us squirming around on the chaise-longue in the living-room one evening, with *Lord of the Flies* on TV, and told us to put the light on. He scowled at me for some time afterwards, and warned me uncomfortably about pregnancy.

Dear Suzy, do you think it's right that we should fuck? I mean we're not all that old. I'm not saying I don't want to, but wouldn't we be breaking all the rules? aw, fuck the rules, let's do it anyway.

Kate advised Chris that we should try oral sex first, but we'd already decided to fuck, after our exams so as not to interfere too much with our studies (in case the earth moved and everything changed, changed utterly).

> *Dear Suzy, why don't we ever get to talk*
> *anymore? I never seem to get my homework*
> *done in time to call, since your father doesn't*
> *like phone-calls after 11. hey, I dig you,*
> *every itty-bitty, teensy-weensy, inbetweeny*
> *thing about you. I love you like dogs like*
> *parks, like meat likes salt, like rain likes*
> *rivers, and I am going to fucking miss you*
> *when you go.*

My imminent departure added a tragic urgency to my romantic life. Our grieving father had accepted an Art History job at Oxford, to add exile to injury.

A few days before what was left of my family was due to leave the country, Chris and I took our bicycles and a condom to the overgrown underbrush of the local defunct loony-bin. I pulled down my jeans and lay before him on some pine needles. Chris stood above me and unzipped his jeans, showing me his penis for the first time. He tried to coax it into action, and said to me, 'You're beautiful.' But his penis was not convinced – I flew to England a virgin.

Not Fran. She and her tall thin boyfriend of Viking descent had deflowered each other a number of times, while claiming to be at the movies.

> First form a tall pointed bud with pink
> Marzipan. Next make a narrow petal by
> tapping a small roll of Marzipan on the
> slab with the finger tip, care being taken

to keep the finger tip dry with powdered
starch. This petal is then fixed to the
bud. Repeat this with another petal.

Ulysses Road   1983

I was sick of artistic rebuffs. I went into the kitchen and made
milky coffee and found the fancy cookies I'd bought for
guests, and took both semi-forbidden delicacies back to my
room. This was where I slept when things with Jeremy were
particularly bad, and where he was always dumping my
junk, like tennis rackets (if I'd had one) and socks and plastic
bags and household additions he didn't like. I sat down at my
little desk, where the papers lay more or less as I'd left them
three days before:

Many artists have used Chance and ready-mades in
order to obscure their exact involvement with the
work of art.

I was supposed to be writing a Ph.D. on collage – I'd decided
to call it 'The Withdrawal Method: the Absence of the
Artist's Touch in Collages and Ready-Mades.' I sighed and
shoved a large succulent scalloped Viennese Finger into my
mouth. It was delicious – how was I going to stop eating
them? I ate four more before deciding that they weren't really
all that good, and managed to throw the tiny corner of one
I'd been holding at mouth level into the waste-basket. An air-
plane flew overhead and my desk-lamp dimmed curiously at
the same time. I wondered when Jeremy would be getting
home.

This study will trace the theme of the artist's non-
participation in the art-making process, through

his/her use of borrowed materials, often merely stuck onto the canvas with glue. The spectator is left to await the artist's return like a bewildered dog at a graveside: hence the claim that Art is Dead.

Ho hum. I decided to consult the TV guides. On one page an irritatingly good-looking woman was displayed inside a sweater which had apparently been doused with Woolite at some stage. But I was instantly rewarded for enduring the woman's charms: the ad included a 20p coupon for Woolite! What other coupons had I been missing all these years? Sure enough, the next page had a good one for an inedible brand of jam – 30p off if you bought two jars. The thought struck me that the world might be my oyster if I just paid more attention.

Clarifying wine (collage) – It is necessary to clarify (coller) wine that is going to be bottled. The purpose of the collage is to give the wine its limpidity.

I put on my favorite radio program, which consisted of a Marriage Guidance counsellor who sat in a studio awaiting phone-calls from people worried about sexual, emotional, or marital problems. I lay down on the floor beside old pieces of Tippex.

Blitzschnelle Korrectur von Tippfehlern.

And now we go to Ann. Are you there, Ann?

Oh, hello, Doctor!

Um, I'm not a doctor, actually. I'm here to discuss or talk through any sexual, emotional or marital problems you might have. How can we help you today, Ann?

Oh, thank you, Doctor. Well, what I'm ringing about, you see, is I live on my own with my little boy. He's ever so good really, I mean, you know, he sees his father and that. We're separated but you know, it's amiable. He gives us money regular, no problem there.

I'm glad to hear it, Ann. Now, what was it you wished to speak to us about right now?

Oh. Well, we have a nice flat, it's not big, you know, but it's very nice. And my mum, she doesn't live with us or anything, but she's just round the corner, and she's just got herself ever such a nice little puppy, and my son is ever so good with it, playing and the like.

Could you tell me how old he is, Ann?

The pup? Oh, he's –

No, I meant your son, Ann.

Oh, my son! Oh, he's five, yeah, five last March.

So what is it you're ringing us about today, Ann?

Well, the thing is, you see, he's such a good little boy, he really is, um, *usually*, but, um, you see, he um plays with himself sometimes. And I'm at the end of my tether, I don't know *what* to do about it!

The whole family could self-destruct for all I cared. Male problems are so dull – always something to do with the penis, either active or inactive. Maybe female problems too. At any rate, I fell asleep without waiting to hear Brian's answer, and didn't wake up until a rousing ad for beds came on:

37

BEDS! BEDS! BEDS! COME ON DOWN. IF YOU NEED A NEW BED, YOU NEED US. 'RELY-ON'! 'SILENT NIGHT'! 'REST EASY'! 'WAVE CREST'! 'TURTLE-DOVES'! 'CUTY-PIE'! 'PRETTY-PLEASE'! ALL THE BEST NAMES, AT THE BEST PRICES! AHHHHHHHHHHHHHHHHHHHH

The voice trailed off in a mock snooze. I fingered the dusty carpet, half-alive.

And now we go to Jane. Jane, are you there? Are you there, Jane?

Hello. Brian?

Yes, I'm here now, Jane. Sorry we had to cut you off for the News. Now, what can we do for you?

I haven't had sex with my husband for two years.

You haven't had sex for two years. Ah. Could you tell me a bit about your husband, Jane?

Well, he's very quiet. I can't think of anything else to say about him really.

What does *he* say about this problem? Have you ever discussed it with him?

Yes. He just says it's because we don't talk enough.

Do you cuddle at all?

Sometimes he gives me a little pat, but if I try to touch *him*, he'll try to get away, like he'll say he's busy or tired or sick or something.

My weeping made Brian's solution inaudible.

A wine cellar must be kept scrupulously clean. No rubbish should be left in it, no vegetables with a strong odor (carrots, onions, cabbage, turnips), no cheese, no barnyard animals.

I could hear Jeremy coming up the stairs, so I turned off the radio. He went straight into the front room to deposit the second-hand briefcase I'd bought him at a jumble sale and decorated with his initials in gold enamel paint back in the days when I loved his every bodily process.

He looked in on me.

'Do you want a cup of coffee?' he asked.

'No, thanks, just had one.'

'Everything okay? Must get on. A lot of papers to mark tonight.'

'Uh, Jeremy, I'm sorry, but I just don't know what I'm doing here.'

'What *do* you mean?'

'Well, we never go out anymore, we hardly ever see each other. We go to bed at different times. I don't know. You're always in the front room . . .' It was a half-hearted effort, like Samson's first '*je t'aime*' (Dalila urges him to say more; I shut up).

'Look, could we possibly talk about this another time? I'll be up all night if I don't get started on this marking.'

I tried to be extra nice all evening after that, relieved that at least I hadn't brought up the lack-of-sex issue. And when he came to bed at about 4.00, he woke me by putting a cold hand between my legs. He was soon fucking me (I didn't attempt to get my cap for fear of his losing interest). Immediately afterwards, he got off me, turned on the light, opened a carton of yoghurt he'd brought with him, and a thriller. I went back to sleep slowly, feeling envious of the yoghurt.

At 10.00 p.m. Gwendoline thinks she sees a ghost and Gertrude thinks she sees a ghost.

What kind of ghost do you think Gwendoline sees and what kind of ghost do you think Gertrude sees? Which girl sees the nicest ghost?

The next day I felt much cheered by this nocturnal event, and to preserve this mood as long as possible thought it wise to be out of the house before Jeremy woke up and ignored me. I would go to the Library to pursue corroboration of my wacky notion of artistic aloofness. My body felt a bit like a ready-made itself, only partially under my control. I deposited it onto a bus, lugged it off again, heaved it towards the British Museum, tried to slide it discreetly across the foyer floor while locating its entry card, and finally plopped it down on a blue leather chair in front of some reserved books.

Before you skin the fish, kill it by banging its head hard against a stone.

'Réponds, réponds à ma tendresse!'

SUSPENDED ANIMATION

How fast we go! The fields, the woods, the bridges seem to fly by so quickly. Soon we'll pass through another strange town at full speed.

Our home town is a very pretty place. The new street-cars share the road with the many automobiles, and there's lots of fine people living here.

Oxford   1970

Not only did the telephone-books look different. Like the end of childhood that it was, England turned out to be tawdry. Scones, lardy-cakes, eccles cakes, the rightly famous English reserve, their taste for the mundane, their pride in the postal system, the lingering memories of ration-books and their resigned acceptance of unhappy occurrences, did not give me confidence. I soon discovered that they pronounced controversy, Caribbean, Connecticut, Michigan and Chicago wrong, and decided to hold on to my American accent through thick and thin.

I, Suzy Schwarz, love and lover of Christopher Taft, sister of my sister, daughter of my father, have hereby decided to end my life and to, therefore, prepare my humble Will.

41

I was using the word, 'therefore', a lot at the time. I lay back, thought of England, and tried to die. I woke to find Franny reading my will.

> *Dear Suzy, I don't want to hear any*
> *more talk about killing yourself.*
> *It would be a terrible loss to the*
> *world, and to your family. Cheer up!*
> *Make friends! Don't be sad.*
>   *I'm sitting here thinking of you,*
> *how I'd like to feel your soft warm*
> *body against mine. I love you!*
>   *By the way, my parents say I*
> *can't come visit you next summer*
> *because they haven't got the money.*

Oxford High School for Girls was a shock to both Franny and me. The British don't like their children distracted from academic achievements by love (it can wait). Franny worked furiously, in order to get her exams over with as soon as possible and get to university. I had four years of sexless education in front of me, and went into a decline.

It was in Oxford that the secret eating began in earnest: I caught Franny hovering around the fridge with suspicious frequency and started to copy her. My hips soon seemed enormous in their circumference. It was all a great revenge on Daddy, fascinated as he was by his own repugnance towards Rubens' women.

> In Poussin's 'Rape of the Sabine Women', as opposed to Rubens' depiction of the same subject, the women are truly unwilling to be abducted. Poussin maintains the seriousness of the situation by surrounding the victims of the outrage with all the arguments against it: parents and children, homes and husbands.

I started sleeping in my school uniform, so as not to have to expend any energy on changing my clothes. Finding me thus clad one morning, Daddy woke me from then on by calling outside my door. At school, I wore a duffle-coat all day, hiding my body from inspection – a hot thing to do in summer, by which time I was also wearing a white woolen hat with two pompoms.

> Gwendoline and Gertrude are buying
> new umbrellas for their trip to England.
>
> Which umbrella will Gwendoline
> choose?
>
> Which umbrella will Gertrude choose?
>
> Which girl chooses the better umbrella?

It was still dark when I got up, gathered books together, and went downstairs to insert as much breakfast into myself without Daddy noticing as possible. No letters, as per usual. I hauled my strange bicycle with its tiny, wearisome wheels which I'd originally considered cute, the whole thing olive-green in memory of Chris's olive-green bicycle (not one of its best features actually), out of the house and rode it down deserted alleyways. Fog or inner gloom obscured everything, as per usual.

I locked my bike in the bicycle shed with other bikes and walked into the school with other girls, but this was the limit of our togetherness. Unlike them, I went straight into Assembly, still wearing my coat and hat, as per usual, the teachers having searched in vain for a rule which forbade the incessant sporting of a hat and coat. During hymn-singing, to which I did not contribute, I noticed an ugly bug crossing the floor under several people's feet. I reckoned its chances of survival, once everyone started filing out, as about nil, and did nothing. I felt blank, as per usual.

43

When you come to America I'm going to
make you stay at our house, every night I'm
going to sneak into your room and make love
with you until dawn. We'll get some hash
and you'll get so stoned you're just lying on
the bed saying 'Love me do'. Later on, we'll
go downtown and meet Melanie who will
otherwise beat me up for keeping you all to
myself.

By the time I got back to Champaign–Urbana, Chris was
distant. He tried at first to avoid me, and then to pretend he
was merely a friend. Melanie said, 'You *have* gotten fatter,
haven't you?' They'd both been reading too many of my
letters. I flew to England a virgin yet again.

In our second year in Oxford, Daddy married Saskia, a
fashion consultant. They thought highly of each other. She
was noticeably gorgeous and clearly considered me a large
blob on her horizon, as did I. Her kisses always landed
somewhere in the air, while a few pointed finger-tips gingerly
made contact with my shoulders. She was fortunately away a
lot, deciding next year's colors.

Saskia is here at the moment – life is
almost unbearable. Tonight she was really
giving us the routine. She said she was in
the way (to which we could only reply to
the contrary) and was going up to bed. We
all had to yell for her to stay down with
us and she said to me: 'You go ahead and
talk to your father.' This was because I'd
been talking to him and not her. So I had
to say: 'Oh, no. I want to talk to you too!'
So at last she came back into the room, and

44

said: 'Well, if you want so much to talk to me, I wish you'd tell me what you got so angry at Daddy about this evening.' So I just said I couldn't remember but it was either because Daddy had yelled himself, or simply because he'd made me angry. Of course it hadn't been much of a quarrel at all, and Saskia's saying that insulted me because at the moment I'm feeling better disposed towards him than ever and a week ago I would have felt her comment was justified but now wouldn't and didn't. Saskia went on to say how 'isn't it too bad' that people get so angry all the time and sometimes hardly realize they might be hurting 'others'. That over, she went on to compliment my clothing: 'That's a very nice skirt, Susan. Where does it come from?'

'India.'

'What, dear?' Her hearing gets bad when she disapproves of something.

'India.'

'Oh, does it really? Very nice. But I don't like that raggedy jumper. And I *hate* that old coat you wear.' She was about to give it away to a charity shop last week. Anyway, then she said I'd wanted a talk with her and that's what she'd given me.

Daddy didn't seem to mind Saskia's long absences. He was immersed in the aesthetic theories of Félibien (Poussiniste) and Roger de Piles (Rubéniste), and in learning to say 'tomaatto', 'Edinbrah', and 'Sinjun' (St John).

At the wedding reception, an old friend of Daddy's asked me if I were happy in Oxford. Daddy piped up cheerfully,

45

'Oh, Suzy will never be happy.' That seemed to sum things up satisfactorily for the bridegroom. I mixed vodka and champagne and was pretty sick.

THE SINKIANG FAT-TAILED SHEEP

I was in the library at school and suddenly I threw over the table and went out the door that exits on to the roof. I didn't know what to do and I was scared so I jumped off and killed myself on the pavement below. The girls inside were a bit startled but were beginning to settle down and when they heard that I was dead, a girl at the table I was sitting at said, 'Well, I'm glad!' – because I had knocked the inkwell on to her clothes when I overturned the table.

> THE MUSK-DEER inhabits the
> steep slopes of the Himalaya.
> He lives an active but lonely
> life and feeds on grass and
> lichens.

After two years of being denied decent parts in Shakespeare on account of my accent, I still had no idea what hydras, enclosures, logarithms, or O-Levels were, and succeeded in proving it, though I astounded my class-mates by passing English Language: they didn't think Americans *knew* the English language. Meanwhile, I drew in pencil all over my bedroom walls in a way that convinced Franny, on one of the occasions when she was exercizing her Unlimited Borrowing Capacity, that I had artistic potential.

> Franny is always stealing my underpants or taking
> my clothes and jewelry without my permission.

46

She doesn't want me to have an identity of my own. I have to hide things I really like when she's at home.

She's always telling me what to do with my life. Now she wants me to go to art school because she didn't get to go. But I think she just doesn't want me to go to university because that's for *her*.

Franny was at the Courtauld, studying Art History. To make a little extra money, she started doing cleaning work. At a particularly grubby flat she caught scabies, and developed a staphylococcus infection in her hand. I caught the infection just by listening to her on the subject over the phone. We both made numerous trips to our respective hospitals to have our putrefying flesh dressed. But even though Franny claimed she rather enjoyed painting herself all over with the pink stuff which was its only cure, I resisted catching scabies.

Just occasionally, I took some control over my own life and did things Franny *hadn't* done (I was the first to get my hair cut at Vidal Sassoon's). And one day, while awaiting my prescription for antibiotics at Boswell's Drug Co., I wandered off to Boots and stole 36p's-worth of make-up. I didn't wear make-up – they were just good objects for practising shop-lifting skills. I was taken to the police station where they photographed and finger-printed me, described my hair on a form as 'mousy', locked me in a cell after removing all my jewelry except the unnoticed toe-ring, and generally made the most of the fact that I was seventeen and therefore arrestable.

When I was delivered home in a certain amount of rehabili-tative distress, Daddy told me he'd stolen things too as a boy, but had been lucky enough not to get caught. He collected my prescription and found me a solicitor, who charged £25 to get me off a £20 fine.

I got a two-year suspended sentence with probation and

psychiatric care, because my lawyer had noticed I was depressed (especially about getting arrested). An Oxford boy of the same age got the same sentence the same week for knifing a fifteen-year-old.

My shrink, slumping puffily behind his sleek desk, asked me if I masturbated, and if I was going to shop-lift again. I answered 'yes' and 'no' in appropriate places once a fortnight. The Probation Officer worked on my depression: she took me on rather long car-drives to scenic spots like Minster Lovell, and back.

EROS VS. THANATOS

Jeremy and I were trying to write a romantic novel, to make ends meet. I gave it up quite soon – the dialogue eluded me – but Jeremy ploughed on, inventing moonlit settings and glam characters late into the night.

> With a piece of yellow Marzipan, roll out
> five thin stamens. Now take some pale pink
> Marzipan and make a narrow petal and fix
> this on to a base. Three more petals are
> made and fixed so that they interlock and
> form a trumpet in the centre of which is
> fixed the bunch of stamens.

In the early days after I'd moved in, Jeremy used to take me on walks around Hampstead, or the Heath, or through the cemetery behind Fortune Green. Mostly new graves. Through it we reached rather posh suburbia which I liked – wealth, quiet, the right to have trees growing along the streets. Jeremy scoffed at it all.

We generally split up on the way home. Jeremy liked to dawdle among the tomb-stones with an eye for a joke, and his expression was almost lecherous when he discerned an unwitting faux-pas or a goofy prayer. I preferred to go home ahead of him and secretly eat something.

This burial ground needs Gardeners
to ensure that rampant growth does
not topple tombs.

At forty, Jack had a loving wife, three adjusted
kids, and his research was considered brilliant. All
these things had no effect, however, on what Jack
called his 'growing deadness'.

I started him on self-monitoring; he was to keep
a graph of how depressed he was each day. This
appealed to Jack's scientific mind.

By the end of ten weeks, Jack's problem was
gone, and he stopped treatment. About a year and
a half later, he telephoned me to say that occasionally he does get the feeling of deadness, but
manages to bring it under control with monitoring.

1973

Franny had first met Jeremy when he was at the Courtauld
doing an M.A. on Cézanne, though he was actually into sex,
drugs and the Rolling Stones at the time (I always felt I'd
missed his prime). They had a brief affair. Franny made her
first joint for him, and they were both sick for a week. She
never smoked dope again. But he was most remembered for
making her turn down a date for the opera with some dishy
guy.

I never failed to trust Franny's enthusiastic appraisals of her
current boyfriends, and longed for these tried and tested
specimens of male perfection myself, though by the time she
broke up with them, they had usually turned out not to be
the crème de la crème after all but had in fact wrecked her
birthday, or her blender. Only occasionally would she hand
one on without too much blackening of character.

She told me she'd been well-pleased with Pietro Fortuni whilst studying Italian under him in Florence. So when Daddy sent me to study Italian in Florence, Franny encouraged me to check Pietro Fortuni out. I found him still eager to take all compliant pubescent pupils to bed, so I gave him a call.

> This is the joy of owning the
> world's first porcelain and crystal
> bell. Impressively wedding the two
> artistic mediums most cherished by
> collectors.
> And wonderfully affordable at
> just £48, payable in convenient
> monthly instalments.

I arrived at his villa in Fiesole, a little disheveled from the perpendicular climb. Pietro Fortuni filled a glass with Pernod on ice for me, and took a smaller one for himself (preserving his faculties). He showed me a glass case full of ugly little glass animals, including a miniscule pig with a visible litter of piglets inside it. He then took me out onto the verandah to show me the orchard of olive trees below. His arm around my shoulders was exciting. He declared that what he liked to do at this time of day (early evening) was to lie down out there on the verandah and watch all the birds flying overhead to the olive trees for the night: he was clearly dependent on a seduction scenario which had served him adequately in the past. So he went off to get the mat. He laid it down and told me to recline on it. I hesitated, thinking of the probable appearance of my fat thighs were I to do so.

'Don't be embarrassed,' he said. 'Here, I'll show you.' He lay down on the mat. I figured that seeing me from below was not going to be much more alluring than how I would look lying down, so I lay down. Pietro Fortuni extended an arm to cushion my head. I contemplated the proffered sky and commented that the birds weren't flying homewards in the anticipated direction. Then we both turned our heads at right angles to our bodies and kissed.

After a reasonably thorough introductory period on the terrace, Pietro Fortuni dragged me off the mat and led me indoors to his bedroom. Napoleon had once owned Pietro Fortuni's bed, or slept in it, or at least sat on it. Pietro Fortuni swiftly took off his clothes, except for his socks, and then undressed me, uttering little compliments here and there. Some ardent pummelling ensued, continually interrupted by the telephone, which Pietro Fortuni bounded off to answer in the living-room – this must have been the reason for the socks. He spouted lively Italian into the receiver. By his second or third disappearance, he took with him the unexciting and unnoticed gift of my virginity, thus adding me to his collection of charmless animals. He fucked another orifice or two, and then dumped me at a bus-stop outside Florence. I've always associated the event with Napoleon.

> The life-like richness of hand-
> painted porcelain, the magic of
> lead crystal, brought together
> as never before.

Another of Franny's offerings was Gonzales, a Nicaraguan refugee. He'd heard of me through Franny and came over to have help on the English in a pamphlet he'd written about the Sandinistas. Franny had told me he was a great lover – and of course I wanted to do what I could for the cause. He started kissing me almost immediately, with a scaly armadillo-like tongue that Franny hadn't mentioned. The Sandinista guerrillas were left to their own devices (consciousness-raising and camouflage, as far as I could ascertain) as he unzipped his jeans in order to reveal a prick that stood straight up like a seventeen-year-old's. He fucked like a seventeen-year-old too, coming, and going, within ten minutes. He never spoke to me again – must have been scaling his contact with foreigners down to a minimum.

'I can't get no satisfaction.'

34a, The Close, Canterbury   1975

Fat, with frizzy, mousy hair and baggy clothes, I morosely massaged the cold gray substance before me until it was so smooth I could no longer feel it. I liked this damp, complacent flesh. I moulded webbed feet, wings, an elephant's trunk, an angular skull, a dinosaur's tail: I'd made another monster.

With some effort, Franny had persuaded Daddy to let me go to art school, and me that I wanted to go. Saskia wondered why I didn't study fashion, but I concentrated on sculpture, and of course Art History.

Daddy and Saskia came to visit me, worried about why I was so depressed. They'd become more or less aware that I was barely attending the art school (designed to be turned into a factory if need be), drinking a lot of dry vermouth, and taking only children's books out of the library. We drove to a fairly fancy pub they'd spotted on their way into town, and ordered Sunday lunches. The food arrived, and I was just about to start eating it, when Daddy said, 'You know, you'd be a lot happier if you lost some weight.'

The food stuck in my throat after that. I couldn't bear to be seen stuffing my fat face. Instead, I felt like killing my father, but the knife beside my plate wasn't satisfyingly sharp enough. As soon as they dropped me off afterwards, I went to the local shop and bought a loaf of Mother's Pride, thick-sliced, and consumed nine-tenths of it (all rolled into doughballs, minus the crusts), sitting up in bed in my bed-sit. I thought of making some noodles after that, but felt too sick to get up.

A girl has to avoid her father between the age of puberty and the time of her marriage. If they meet in the road, she hides while he passes, and she may never go and sit near him.

GWENDOLINE AND GERTRUDE

Ulysses Road   1983

'But what I want to know is, what shall I do about my tubers?'

'I've always been fascinated b–'

I switched the radio off – somebody's always been fascinated by something. Skirting round the white slabs of overcooked noodle, the semi-dissolved tomatoes and the pyramidal remains of potatoes, I was searching for what was left of the cauliflower (under the mistaken belief that cauliflower has some nutritional value), and nearing the conclusion that I'm not much of a cook, when the phone rang.

'Oh, Susan, dear, how are you?' Saskia, at her most alarmingly effulgent. I responded with my customary reserve.

'I'm eating soup. How are you?' I felt she would somehow know I was eating something, in fact that was probably why she'd called, so I thought I might as well admit it.

'Oh, very well, my dear. Can't talk long, I'm afraid. I'm just calling to give you some exciting news!' Pause, so that I would have to ask, 'What news?'

'What?' I asked.

'Well, you know your father's friend, Jill? Oh, of course you do, you met her at that little do of ours. Susan? Are you still there, Susan?'

'Yeah. Yes, I know Jill.'

'Well, she has a friend at the University of Utah.' Another pause. Was this supposed to interest me?

'Oh, does she?'

'Yes. And this friend is putting on an Art History conference in Copenhagen and, wait for it, she wants to know if *you* would like to give a talk!'

'WHAT???'

'She wants to know if you'd like to give a talk in Copenhagen!'

'Of course I'd like to! What on? What did you tell her? When do I leave?'

'Oh, your father will have all the details. I just couldn't wait, I *had* to tell you!'

'But I never even – How did she hear of me? Do you know, Saskia?'

'Oh, I don't know much more. You'll have to ask Daddy all that.'

'God, this is incredible. And a friend of mine just asked me to come and stay with him in Copenhagen!'

'Ohhh. *Who?*'

'Now don't get excited. He's gay. *And*, you forget I'm living with Jeremy!'

We giggled in a friendly fashion about this and then said goodbye. I had definitely lost my cool with Saskia, but it seemed to please her, which she suddenly seemed to deserve. Brushing this perplexing development aside, I spent the night surveying the glorious future spreading before me: international renown. I tried to think up a topic to lecture on. 'Aloofness, from Chardin to Christo.' 'Artistic Absence and Abstinence.' 'Fake Ready-Mades, from Oldenburg to Louise Nevelson.' 'Why Claes Oldenburg Doesn't Do His Own Sewing.' 'Yoghurt-Buying in Modern Britain.'

I called my father in the morning. He enquired about my financial affairs, which he often alleviated, the state of my car, which he'd given me, and the progress of my Ph.D., which he had some hopes of my finishing. After receiving fairly optimistic appraisals of all three, he seemed about to hang up, so I had to say, 'Uh, Daddy, I was just wondering, do you know anything about a friend in Utah, I mean a friend of *Jill*'s in Utah? Saskia said she maybe wanted me to give a talk–'

'Oh, it's *Fran* they want! I don't know where Saskia got the idea it was *you*. So silly!'

'ah.'

'I'm sorry she told you . . .'

'No, that's okay. I'll recover. I, Uh, just wanted to see Sweden, that's all.'

'Denmark.'

'What?'

'Did you say Sweden?'

'Is Copenhagen in Denmark?'

'Yes.'

'Oh well, I wanted to go to Sweden, so that's okay.'

Swigging the rest of my tea, I caught a glimpse of my own eye in the shiny bottom of the cup, and quickly looked away.

I took my coupon to the local grocery store. They didn't have any Woolite, but as I was inspecting their range of biscuits, the man in charge crept near me and said, 'You're beautiful.' I pretended not to have heard, giving him the chance to bethink this opinion. I was leaning over the cucumbers when the guy repeated his statement and kissed me on the cheek. Adroitly side-stepping the situation, and the cucumbers, I asked him how you cook baby aubergines, several of which nestled, warming, in my palm. He shrugged, and suddenly looked foolish to me, wandering around after customers while his wife was frying baby aubergines in lemon and garlic for him at home.

BANANA SPLIT

J. O's. Me: £406.34½
              10.00   petrol
               5.00   loan
                .60   stamps
            ─────────
             423.93½
              17.70   paper bill
              24.00   rent + £6
              18.16   party food
               5.00   loan
              12.00   Habitat
              21.00   rent
            ─────────
            £518.77½
               3.00
               2.05?   cigs
            ─────────
            £563.87½

F. O's. Me: £154.49
               2.75
               2.00
              27.94   (½ Daddy's XMAS radio)
            ─────────
            £187.18

            + 1 copy Yeats' poems

(They told me to keep track!)

58

Franny had given my affair with Jeremy at best three years, and thought he was depressing me. Jeremy told me not to let Franny stay too often because she seemed to depress me. Jeremy was in fact the first method I'd found of keeping Franny at bay.

I was thinking about English Central Heating when the DHSS man arrived to check whether Jeremy and I were living together or just cohabiting. The English have adopted Central Heating like some kind of cargo cult, like wooden air-planes in Papua New Guinea or the non-functioning fridges prominently displayed in Russian living-rooms. All the English seem to know is they're supposed to have these sharp-looking metal objects scattered around the walls – they're not interested in heat. But what can one expect in a country where a plug on an electrical device is considered an optional extra? The DHSS man decided we were just living together.

After he'd gone, I sat down and wrote a letter to Chris, with whom I had not bothered to communicate for twelve years:

> *Dear Chris,*
>   *Sorry not to have been in touch*
> *for twelve years. Sorrier than you may*
> *imagine, in fact. I can't get you*
> *out of my system. Please come fuck*
> *me soon so I can see you're no better*
> *than other men. Come soon.*
>   *I'm living with a guy who likes*
> *crisps and yoghurts in bed when he*
> *has a cold. He treats me well whenever*
> *I'm sick and brings me Lemsip, but*
> *immediately feels very hard-done-by*
> *and gets sick himself and needs crisps*
> *and yoghurts brought to him.*

I'm writing a Ph.D. but not getting
it done. I lie on the floor listening
to hard-luck stories on the radio.
Recently I retrieved the shoe-box full of
your letters, from our house in Oxford.
How could you have loved me so much?
Come fuck me soon.

That done, I decided to take a walk on Hampstead Heath. It was twilight, with a bright thin crescent moon low in the sky. Joggers passed, no muggers, so I went deeper. I sat on a bench in order feel all alone in the dark. I almost managed this before the cold and the fear began to dominate.

I got up. It was very dark as I began to move. Aiming as well as I could for the dimly recollected route I'd come by, I caught sight of a dark form like me on a bench not far off, and became convinced that this person, unlike me, was a psychopath. I deeply regretted being on the Heath after dark, when it was known to become infested with psychopaths. I acknowledged that I was terrified, aware of my own vulnerability. Feeling very weak but ignoring fatigue and my conspicuous heart-beat, I walked very fast uphill. Darkness and tiny sounds. I cut across a field hoping it would lead somewhere and that no psychopath would notice me marching across open terrain. I squelched through soggy grass, hearing the sound of water trickling everywhere.

My aim was good: I came out near Kenwood House, that bastion of decency, and marched out into the lighted street with a great sense of my own strength and resilience.

Several strong cords are fixed to this and
these are fixed to a special harness.

I registered defeat: Franny would be impossibly self-congratulatory now about the shopping expedition. She'd actually gotten me to try on and buy several articles of clothing I'd probably never have the guts to wear.

'Okay, now let's go have a drink,' I said, lugging the semi-welcome bags out of the shop.

'Nope. Time for ice-cream!' declared Franny, steering me off Oxford Street towards a fairly Americanized ice-cream parlor within sight. Franny sure knew how to have a good time.

She ordered a Hot Fudge Sundae, emphasizing her interest in a lot of cream and a lot of hot fudge and anything else the establishment might think of plopping on. Still her favorite, I noted: Hot Fudge. Fearing her equally familiar displeasure if I didn't join in her brand of self-indulgence – the danger of falling into the Gwendoline and Gertrude trap – I ordered a concoction of similar magnitude, though featuring a banana.

The mood was restless as we awaited our ice-cream. I tried to make conversation:

'There was something I wanted to ask you, but I can't remember what. When are you coming to London again, by the way?'

'I hope those sparkly pants are ready in time for Copenhagen,' Franny replied (they were being shortened). 'Where did we get them? That was a good place. Aren't you glad you came? About time you got out of all those terrible baggy things. See? Aren't you having a good time? Well, aren't you?'

'Top Shop.'

Franny began searching frantically for her wallet. I was about to tell her it was on her lap, when her Hot Fudge Sundae arrived. Its purple paper parasol had failed to protect it from a hailstorm of chopped walnuts. Franny sent it back, claiming that she had never agreed to walnuts.

'God!' she exclaimed. 'They still don't know anything about ice-cream in this country.' She craned her neck to see if any innocent bystanders had taken this insult in.

After the walnut contretemps, Franny was even more fidgety. She collected dollops of my undisputed item on her index finger, and then took a spoon to it. I tried to divert her attention with more conversation.

'Hey, leave some of it for me!'

As we delved into the same mound of whipped cream topped with caramel syrup, I quelled my desire to defend my ice-cream with physical force if necessary. Sitting back in a gesture of dog-like submission, I enquired about her man-friend of the moment.

'Oh God, Suzy! He has the most beautiful body. Just wait till you see him! He's so American – big shoulders, big jaw, big everything!' She smirked.

'Really?' I asked, moving closer to my ice-cream.

'But why does he never come?' she asked mournfully.

'What *do* you mean?' I asked, brightening a little with this peculiar revelation.

'With my Hot Fudge Sundae, what did you think I meant, fuck it!' She dropped her spoon on top of my banana affair and almost rose up off her swivel seat.

'God Almighty, why don't you eat some more of *my* thing if you're so hungry,' I offered diplomatically. 'For Christ's sake!' I added.

She looked a bit sheepish then, I thought, and said, 'No, thanks, I don't like yours. I particularly don't like that obscene banana sticking out of it.' The dish was nudged back in my direction.

'Christ,' I said.

Franny's Hot Fudge Sundae returned with merely a cherry on top this time, embedded like a belly-button in a virtuoso whipped cream display. She accepted it. I considered trying to draw her attention to the resemblance of the fudge elements to pubic hair peeking out of frilly white lingerie, but settled instead for a private fantasy in which her order was swiftly deflowered by mine.

62

We were supposed to meet the great Rod, and old Jeremy, at a pub of Jeremy's choosing in Soho. Jeremy had given us the wrong name and the wrong street, or at least one or the other, but somehow Franny and I got there, only about half an hour late. They were hunched over in a corner: Rod was giving Jeremy a detailed description of the production of *Tristan and Isolde* that he and his ex-wife had seen at Bayreuth a few years back. Jeremy was fascinated. No, really – Jeremy loved Wagner (in fact any passive activity that took up a great deal of time).

It was a while before we could complain about being misdirected to the pub.

A SURE METHOD OF REDUCING
WEIGHT WITHOUT DISCOMFORT
Foods to be avoided
Over-fat people nearly always eat too
much fat-building food, particularly
starchy foods, sugar, candies and sweet
desserts. The following articles should
be rigidly excluded from the dietary:
candy, sugar, preserves and sweetmeats
of all sorts, ice-cream, sweet desserts, fat
meats.

Write for a free copy of our
comprehensive booklet:
'Girth Control'

One day I was unable to attend a lecture at the Courtauld given by an Impressionism expert famous for his frequent use of the phrase, 'throwing the baby out with the bath-water', because I felt sick. When Jeremy came home and sat down on the bed in which I was lying, I nearly threw up. I was still feeling sick the next day, so I went to the doctor. He suggested a pregnancy test.

'But what about my feeling sick?' I asked.

'The two could be related, you know.' He peered at me.

'But it can't be Morning Sickness! I feel sick all the time!'

It was a shock to Jeremy and me that we were fertile.

> *The Lacto-Dextrin Method*
> It must be remembered that with
> Lacto–Dextrin liberal quantities of
> roughage to supply bulk, and paraffin
> in some form to supply lubrication
> must be taken. Both bulk and
> lubrication are needed.

A WINTER WEDDING

Around the time when Jeremy and Suzy were discussing the significance of her pregnancy and whether or not it should be allowed to continue (Jeremy suggested not, on the grounds that he would feel inclined to love the child and their relationship was too unstable to warrant such a commitment; Suzy suggested continuing the pregnancy, on the grounds that otherwise she would feel inclined to commit suicide), Fran was finding it increasingly hard to reach Rod. Having allowed for the two weeks he was going to be in Germany visiting his ex-wife and child, Fran began calling the Art History Department office. The secretary did her best to head Fran off at the pass, as per usual. Life revolved around this woman's whims. Decisions about salaries and schedules, admin., admissions and assignations, all depended on her likes and dislikes, her long lunch hours. But finally Fran found Rod, shooting his mouth off in the Top Bar, with a tactile young German grad student hanging on his arm.

Rod phoned Fran that night to tell her she hadn't loved him enough: they both agreed that the break-up was all her fault. She avoided all three university bars after that. It was agony to meet him, and he was always somewhere, seeking out a new ear for an old story. She was amazed he ever got anything done. She, by contrast, devoted herself to non-stop work on her long-awaited, already-advertised book, *The Con-Artist Exposed: Violence and Humiliation Committed in the*

Name of Art. She believed, like her father, that scholarship was the only antidote to emotional turmoil.

Rod however had no respect for such artificial divisions between one's work and personal life. An article called 'Mauling the Material: Auto-Destructive Art and Artists', appeared in *D.K. Magazine* (short for 'Dependable Kerchief') a few weeks later, under the name of Roderick J. J. McMead.

> Fairly deep drawers are more useful than shallow ones. It is essential that the bench be very rigidly constructed. It need not necessarily be fixed to the floor, but it should be supported against the wall at the back. Its structure should be braced so that it does not yield under the pressure of heavy filing or chipping, or other strenuous operations. It is better not to make the bench too low, to avoid stooping. A firm, solid work-bench is a necessity, as well as a comfort, when working.

When I told Franny I was pregnant, she said, 'You idiot!' No one could believe I wanted it, and of course the thought had only just occurred to me too: I had considered it perfectly natural that the lovelessness of adolescence would be followed by the childlessness of contemporary adulthood. But my father offered to support me and the baby and, to my surprise, seemed to consider this new development of greater importance than my Ph.D.

If I was going to commit suicide as the result of an abortion, I would have to have the baby, it was decided by Jeremy. And seeing as how we loved each other so much, he asked me to marry him – I agreed to both plans. I was no longer of this world. My mind focused on the huge will to exist of the tiny bunch of cells multiplying inside me every day.

For fear of people thinking we were only getting married because I was pregnant, I wanted the wedding to be as soon as possible. We were therefore married about six months before my condition became at all noticeable – within three weeks of the diagnosis. While Saskia stifled a tear, Franny silently fretted, and a crowd of Jeremy's diffident brothers shuffled a crowd of feet, he and I declared some kind of eternal togetherness.

We drove out of Oxford for our honeymoon: a night in Woodstock. We stayed at an old inn which seemed unnecessarily fancy. The fridge was stuffed with the rudiments of a cocktail party which did not occur during our occupancy. We were summoned into a fairy-tale parlor for supper, everything lavishly encumbered with flowery cloth and crêpe paper, as if serious attention had been given to the dampening of acoustics, or the possibility of our slopping the soup. The other hotel guests, already seated and wearing party hats, watched us come in. We all got two crackers each. It was New Year's Eve.

The meal was elaborate. I wasn't hungry. Jeremy finished my profiteroles. We went for a stroll afterwards, and got cold. Neither of us admitted to feeling observed, on show, on honeymoon. We went back to our room and sat on the bed. Jeremy taught me how to play poker with the tiny cards I'd gotten in a cracker. Then we consummated the business of the day. I went to sleep. Jeremy lay awake, contemplating minor faux-pas he'd committed.

The next morning, we took a walk through the grounds of Blenheim Palace, right past a dead body that wasn't discovered until a few days later.

Is your partner away from home at the moment?
Why is your partner away from home?
Have you got a partner living with you?
What is your relationship to your partner?

Married ☐
Living together ☐

What is your marital status?

Single ☐
Widowed ☐
Divorced ☐
Separated ☐

If you are not sure what to tick, please explain here:

TENDRESSE

If individual molds are used, place one teaspoon clear jelly in bottom of each. When nearly firm, place on it one tablespoon mayonnaise. When this is firm fill molds with salad mixture. Chill until firm.

For the first time since my efforts to get hold of peanut-butter-and-jelly sandwiches in childhood, I saw in pregnancy a chance to feel Normal. I went to ante-natal clinics and had blood tests and urine analyses, I was asked questions about myself, I was scanned with ultra-sound and saw my child's back through technological mists. My body could do this incredible thing, just like everybody else.

I talked with strangers about pregnancy and discovered that I had physical and emotional experiences in common with other women. I exploited the fact that one need only say one is pregnant to get a seat on a tube, or access to a loo. A now queenly vessel, in my own opinion, I was affronted when people didn't shift themselves in order to accommodate me. My comfort was suddenly of universal importance: my womb gave me rights on this earth.

I loved going to the Breathing Classes, where birth was seen as emotionally stupendous, and everyday – simultaneously. I couldn't get enough of it. In fact I enrolled for an extra and rather inferior private class in Pregnancy, in which we did little exercises and were ordered never to stand with our legs straight and knees locked – they should always be a little bent, as if one is about to pounce.

Baby-care was of course never mentioned. No one had the audacity to suggest the practicalities surrounding pregnancy's product (not because it would all be easy after that, but where would the advice end – toilet-training, adolescence, UCCA forms?). Everything but our breathing was left to us, or to chance. I never even mastered the breathing. It was pregnancy alone that was the issue, and we were all excited about it (mothers of previous children perhaps less so). It was a pleasure only appropriate to share with other pregnant people, and yet I wanted Jeremy to come to the classes to learn how to be a Labor Partner (he didn't). I wanted to have a Natural Birth (I didn't). I wanted the baby to come (she did).

The woman we'd all cheerfully encircled, each holding a plastic cup of free tea, had told us, 'We don't call them "pains" any more, we call them "contractions".'

The pain was unbearable. I wanted my Mommy. I was all alone in a strange cruel country with an alien being tearing around inside me (what was I doing having a baby in England anyway?). No one seemed to consider my predicament disturbing or unfortunate. No one even believed I was in labor. Jeremy was sent home – 'false alarm' – while I clenched my teeth in a prenatal ward, wrecking the goodnight's-sleep of six-months' pregnant women fearing miscarriages or still-births or feet-first deliveries.

The nurse who gave me an internal examination during a contraction said, 'Don't cry – it'll just tire you out.' I cried. Another nurse suggested a bath, another told me to walk around. Extremely clean, I toured the fourth floor of the dark hospital in agony, clinging to walls and window-sills. I returned to the nurses who, having agreed that I was in labor, arranged for me to go down to the Labor Ward for an epidural.

The lift wasn't working. The lift-man said, 'Lucky it's not an emergency.' I informed him that it was. Two floors down, I writhed on a bed for ten minutes, and then froze effortfully while an anaesthetist inserted a needle into my spine. I no longer feared paralysis, only pain. When the epidural took effect, I was plunged into an ecstasy of non-pain. At this point Jeremy turned up. It was clear to all present that he was not needed, so he went off to have a sleep in the waiting-room while I dilated.

My only sense of communion with the outside world during labor came from Hieronymus Bosch, for having imagined obstetrical hell before me. When the baby's head lodged in my vagina, I assumed rather pessimistically that we would remain like that forever. The midwife urged me to be slow and gentle, but I secretly(?) pushed. Jeremy watched. A huge object – a tiny human body – slowly emerged from mine, and was placed on the belly that had kept it safe. She looked at me with dark, alert eyes. A distinctive face of her own, but dark hair like my mother's. I loved this person, for such she suddenly seemed to be. I held her to me, I fondled the new little legs and arms, and the back that I already knew. At last I could touch her – at last I could love someone. A ferocious summer storm raged outside the already darkened room, as if the gods (or goddesses) acknowledged the significance of this birth. I said 'Hello'.

My intense thirst for cherry juice proved a tall order for Jeremy, who kept turning up with substitutes, and in-laws. Daddy thought the sign on the door of the Maternity Ward – 'Fathers not allowed after 7.30' – was meant for him. So he came during the day-time, repeatedly, to see the baby he alone had encouraged me to have, and asked me how I knew which one was mine. He lay down on my bed and slept.

Nurses and porters brought cups of tea. I was taught how to change a nappy. The mothers talked, took frequent salt

71

baths, used soft sanitary pads, ate numerous eggs and vegetables, and commiserated with those who'd had Caesarians.
The room was full of babies, and I was overwhelmed with
love for them all.

After a week of this Jeremy took me home. In a burst of
hormonally inspired energy a few months before, I had
found our house after tramping through about fifty others
(Irving didn't want any miniature tenants). It had been the
only one Jeremy liked, so with my father's help we'd bought
it. As we approached it now, Jeremy spoke proudly of the
achievements of a carpenter he'd hired during my absence: a
few of the floor-boards I'd machine-sanded and lacquered
while heavily pregnant had been removed and replaced by
somewhat better floor-boards which had yet to be sanded
and lacquered but would of course look great if we ever got
around to it.

TRICYCLE . . .

We'd become a family. Jeremy at once forbade me to have Lily in bed with us, so I slept a good deal on cushions on the floor of the junk-room to which she'd been banished. It spared me having to completely wake up and get cold in order to feed her during the night. And I didn't like to part with her: I missed her when she slept.

Jeremy kept his contact with Lily down to a minimum – he said this kept him refreshed, and made him more careful when he *was* with her. Sometimes he gave her a bath, allowing *me* to get refreshed for a few minutes, but he always needed help finding the tub and a towel and the soap and dry clothes and a nappy for afterwards, and some more help when getting her out of the water, since at such times she was very slippery. Yet, when I accused him of behaving like an uncle, he was offended. He was carrying out the most important parental duty, after all: taking photographs.

Within three weeks of Lily's birth, I was again considering leaving Jeremy. I mentioned this to him. He said, 'Nobody's leaving anybody,' and I was cowed.

I became subdued: suddenly released from the former concerns of my life and exposed to unexpected vistas of deep love, I wanted everything to be perfect, and this was hard to arrange.

I dressed my baby in stripy outfits and fed her almost continually. She had accepted me, and her capacity to tolerate my love was a revelation.

When Lily became quite spherical, Jeremy began to worry about her weight. I began to worry about her father, as he sat there calculating Lily's chances of finding a mate in later life, on the basis of plumpness in early infancy.

I'm breast-feeding Lily. We're surrounded by nappy-changing apparatus and general domestic chaos. Jeremy comes downstairs. He asks: 'Is it all right if I take out the things in the washing-machine so I can wash my clothes?'
I shrug.
When I get up to the bathroom later, I find my failed heap of towels and baby-clothes lying on the floor beneath the machine which gently sudses Jeremy's duds.

> Top it with an aigrette of spun sugar. Decorate
> with preserved cherries glazed in sugar cooked to
> crack stage.

A Health Visitor comes. I welcome her warmly, so happy to see a living person who wants to see me and talk about babies. I'm amazed when she tells me that some people slam the door in her face. I ask her every baby question I can think of, just to keep her there as long as possible.
Jeremy comes downstairs briefly and meets her. Plays the father. Goes back upstairs. Later he asks me what she came for. I act blank.

Everything was going well for Suzy, Fran thought: Married, With A Baby. Jeremy was not perhaps ideal, but still, Married, With A Baby. Fran managed to get a year off to teach at an American art school – she felt a need for Twinkies, Oreos, Pop-Tarts, hamburgers, bagels, lobster, ice-cream, frozen yoghurt, movies, sun, snow, slang, and friendly people.
All the men turned out to be married, all the women single. Her students were indifferent to Art History and,

after the first week or so, the food was just food. Fran got a lot of work done, and sent Suzy a nice green cushion shaped like a fish, and insisted that Suzy make a $50 bet with her that Fran would not meet an interesting, interested man within the next five years.

... THORNS ...

It takes a minimum of three months to regain your figure. Yet the Princess of Wales had to make her first public appearance at the Falklands Thanksgiving Service at St Paul's Cathedral, only a month later. In an off-the-peg dress, tightly belted to emphasize her returning – but not quite returned – waistline, she did not look her best.

When Lily was just beginning to walk, we decided to go to Jeremy's grandmother's old place in Cornwall for a long week-end. We were getting ready to depart. Jeremy was in the bathroom for a long time. I ironed his shirts, and a dress for Lily. I fed her. I dressed her and myself, and packed nappies and a changing-mat and baby lotion and Drapolene and nappy liners and extra baby clothes for mishaps during the drive and anything else I could remember. I hoovered the dining-room, washed the stinking dishes, threw out suspect things in the fridge, cleaned the counters, fed Lily, fed the cat, wrote a note for the cat-sitter and located three cans of cat-food, cleaned out the cat-litter, found a bottle of wine to take (I'd need it), put water in the car radiator while holding Lily (not easy), returned to the house, locked all the windows, turned off the heat, collected packets of crisps for Jeremy to eat on the journey and some bananas for Lily, and fed her again.

At last Jeremy was ready to go. I carried Lily out to the car in her carry-cot and fastened it into the harness while Jeremy positioned his legs and arms in the front seat. He consulted a map briefly and then unfolded his newspaper as I started driving. I informed him of the presence of the crisps.

He said nothing until Liverpool Street, when he asked if I'd double-locked the front door. We drove back and I got out and checked the front door. It was double-locked. We were off, once again. Half-way to Andover, when Lily stirred in her sleep, Jeremy asked me, 'Did you bring any toys for Lily?'

'No. Did *you*?' I dared to reply.

We broke the journey at Longleat. Between the Victorian Kitchen and the School-Girl Uniform exhibition, we found a health-food store where we bought some lemon cheese, handmade in Kent. We experienced the Safari boat-ride: a glide across a small brown lake on a pleasure boat notable for the massive dugong it sported as a mast-head. She took us past some lukewarm seals, a hippo, and three thirty-year-old gorillas stranded on an island.

We paused for a drink at the Longleat arms, where wasps attacked my sandwich and Jeremy's cigar after he and Lily had gone off to check out the penguin and the guinea pigs in the Pet's Pagoda. I took the remaining Guinness, the cigar and the pushchair with its load of health-food to the Ladies'. There was a crush of women and children at various stages of relieving themselves. The ones on the outside of the booths stared at me with my Guinness, cigar, and empty pushchair, with a touch of disgust, I thought. I joined Lily and Jeremy for a ride on the toy-town train, First Class. Surrounded by Oxbridge entrants enamoured with the marijuana they'd smoked at lunchtime, we caught a last glimpse of the gorillas on their island.

We arrived in Mousehole late that night. The self-sacrifices of Jeremy's late grandmother and the morose wood-carving of his late grandfather filled the place with guilt and gloom. I transferred Lily from the car to the old cot, carefully preserving her unconscious state, and soon went to bed myself. A bad picture of Christ, heavily crowned with one of the grandfather's elaborate frames, hung over our bed. I remembered reading *Portnoy's Complaint* in that bumpy bed, and afterwards trying to give Jeremy a blow-job. As ever, my lust had been inconvenient.

Early the next morning, I stomped out of the house, convinced that I didn't care if I lived or died, I forget why. I headed upwards, and found a coastal footpath. I stumbled and skitted along it in thin shoes, more conscious of the layout of the pebbles underfoot than of the enviable proximity of the invisible sea. I thought about drowning myself though, and more and more and more, I needed to shit. It was a cloudy day. It would always be cloudy.

At last I saw a little shed beside the path, hidden behind a lot of foliage. For some reason, I felt it had once been a pig-pen. The perfect place for my purposes. Once inside the pen, I decided the hut itself would make an even better loo. I pulled open what was left of the gate and crouched to get into the shelter. A large piece of tarpaulin lying along the ground inside gave me a funny feeling. The realization that its contours bore some relation to a human form made me want to depart rapidly, but then I thought I ought to check if the person were dead. Suddenly the whole expanse of tarpaulin jerked and I took off, scrambling through vines and twigs and thorns to get away from what I assumed to be a runaway murderer. I didn't feel safe until the path back towards Mousehole had taken several turns, thereby making my flagging but still running body invisible, even if still followable. I returned to the house, feeling how dearly I valued my life.

... BICYCLE

Dear Ms Schwarz,

    Thank you for your letter of 7 February.
I was very sorry that one of our conductors
treated you in the way that you describe
when you tried to board a bus at Piccadilly.
It is true that people are not allowed to
bring unfolded pushchairs onto buses, but
the conductor should have waited whilst you
folded it. I am also sorry to hear that
you subsequently had to hold your rather
hefty offspring for over twenty minutes
before another appropriate bus turned up.
Please accept these chocolate-covered Brazil
nuts as a token of our sincere regret that
these experiences ever happened to you.

My father told me a joke:

    Guy knocks on the door. Old woman answers. Guy says, 'Hello! I'm collecting money for the Kingston Bagpuize/ Stoke Poges Annual Rugby Team Benefit.'

    'What?'

    'Um, I'm collecting money for the Kingston Bagpuize/ Stoke Poges Annual Rugby Team Benefit!'

    'WHAT?'

    'I'M COLLECTING MONEY FOR THE KINGSTON BAGPUIZE/STOKE POGES ANNUAL RUGBY TEAM BENEFIT.'

'*WHAT*???'

'Aw, fuck you.' Turns to go.

'FUCK YOU TOO, and FUCK THE KINGSTON BAGPUIZE/STOKE POGES ANNUAL RUGBY TEAM BENEFIT!'

I was getting ready to tell Jeremy that I didn't want to live with him anymore. I kept up the extremely-cold-shoulder routine for a full week, and had almost reached a plausible explosion point, when Jeremy lost a contact lens. Blind without them. I had to stay with him until he got a new pair. But by then I had struck up a certain momentum, and couldn't quite last out the period compassion called for.

'What do you think is in it for me?' I asked one night, when the subject seemed to me to have arisen. 'All I get out of this relationship is direct access to guilt, martyrdom and low self-esteem. Our neighbors think I'm some kind of prisoner in here!'

'What *do* you mean?' asked Jeremy, not quite grasping it. 'I contribute to the bills! It's not easy for *me*, you know, the fact that *you* own our house. And you're so bloody self-righteous about it all too. Fran's right: you're such a goody-goody, you know that? The only thing I feel I have any claim to around here is the fucking washing-machine!'

'Take your fucking washing-machine.'

'*What did you say?*'

'Nothing.'

'Don't you dare talk to me like that!'

'Don't you dare pull me like that!'

He let go of my wrist and I went over to our bed to get Lily, who'd fallen asleep with a fever. Jeremy tried to pull her away from me, and accidentally bumped her head, making her cry. I pulled her to me, suddenly determined, and ran out of the room. Jeremy grabbed the sleeve of my nightgown, which tore. Sure that my end was nigh if I remained in the house, I ran down the stairs and out the front door and stood outside in the middle of Shoreditch in bare feet and a damaged nightgown holding a two-year-old whose feet were also bare, and thought how only Masaccio could paint the bare bottom of a baby with the right degree of tenderness. It was five in the morning.

Jeremy called me back in after a few minutes, under the mistaken assumption that we'd both calmed down. He said he was sorry, he wasn't himself because of his lack of contact lenses. Jeremy explained himself for an hour or two, while I nursed Lily back to sleep, and then he and I went to bed too. As soon as his breathing seemed reliably slumbrous, I got up, packed some things, wrote a cowardly note about the benefits to us both of a short separation, and bundled the sleeping Lily into the car.

We headed west, which in America would take a week, and in Britain can be accomplished in three hours. By ten in the morning, Lily was riding on a Kiddy-Bounce Rocket at Tintern Abbey, which was a disappointment to us both. We proceeded to the Black Mountains. The Welsh seemed all agreed on keeping their reputation as a melancholy race, and I rather appreciated this. A lot ended up in Patagonia, I gather.

WINE, A RECORD-PLAYER, AND LILY

You'll be able to tackle simple repairs or ambitious projects with complete confidence. From fixing a dripping tap and rewiring a fuse to installing a shower unit and adding a new power circuit.

Fidelity and Security Ltd
request the pleasure
of your company
at a reception
honouring the opening
of our new office

Ideal for recording those important appointments and special days. In full colour throughout it is an attractive and constant reminder of some of the best of the sporting events of the year.

It was messy, it was childish, it was unkind. Finally I'd dared to go, and it was a great relief.

Daddy said he quite understood my leaving Jeremy, and sent me the money to rent a flat in Pimlico until Jeremy found himself somewhere else to live.

Jeremy visited the newly created one-parent family almost daily, and spent more time with Lily than he ever had before.

I acquired a succession of child-minders with varying abilities, and considered my thesis officially resumed:

> In his 'Fountain', Duchamp's personal contributions were heavily disguised. He signed the object (a urinal) with the name, R. Mutt, after selecting it according to his usual procedure – 'the choice was based on a reaction of visual indifference, with a total absence of good or bad taste, in fact a complete anaesthesia.'

Wine, a record-player, Lily, and the proximity of delicatessens helped, as Fran's cast-offs started turning up, unaware that I had secretly vowed never to take on another of them. There was Mick, who claimed to be considering the purchase of my car, which I could no longer afford. I invited him over in friendly if self-seeking fashion. He brought Pouilly Fumé, of which he was rather proud; I didn't like it. After supper, we watched *Newsnight*. I tried to ignore my gloomy, drooping companion, who still mooned over Fran. I thought instead of what I was going to do after he'd left: drink some (other) wine, smoke another joint, maybe have some more of the surprisingly delicious crumble I'd made, which Mick had already eaten most of. A little time to myself before going to bed. Mick roused himself to ask: 'Suzy, do you think I could stay the night? Do you mind?'

'No. No, that's fine. I've got some spare sheets.'

I knew it. I'd been waiting for this all evening. His pathetic ploy for getting into a position to make some sort of pass. Impervious to a hint.

That decided, Mick promptly fell asleep on the chaise-longue. I had to wake him up when I brought him the sheets and blankets. He then asked if I had an extra alarm clock. I said I'd give him mine, which I claimed not to need. He followed me down the hall, where I quickly flicked on the bright white light-bulb which hung unromantically on a cable. He followed me right into my room, where Lily was sleeping. I got tense. Presumably the pass was due at any moment. I hoped Lily's presence, or the messiness of the room, might put him off, depending on which type of squeamishness he cultivated.

I stooped to get the clock and righted myself as swiftly as possible. I then hurried past him into the harsh light of the hall. He started talking about something, while moving towards the other room, before he realized I wasn't coming too. I'd retreated to the door of my bedroom again. He finally got the message and said goodnight. I slept stiffly, full of the triumph of deflecting one of the approved consorts – though I was not convinced that this had been achieved until I heard him lugging his bicycle out of the entrance hall the next morning.

Mick was in bed and asleep within seconds. He woke the next morning refreshed, and pleased that he had stayed at Suzy's place, which almost halved his journey to work. He left as soon as he was dressed, so as to avoid having to make any more conversation with Suzy. She'd become very dull lately. Probably from smoking so much dope. That Jeremy had been a very good influence. Good cook too. Poor Suzy. What a weird apple crumble that was! He wasn't going to take that leaky car either, even for £50.

Another guy thought that intimate disclosures about Franny's sexual idiosyncrasies would be enticing. He took me out for an Italian meal and told me it had once taken him 120 thrusts to make Franny come. I drank a lot of wine and got sloshed enough to have to go straight home, alone, to bed.

There is thus a double deprivation for the spectator: not only is the urinal's aesthetic value in question, but its ability to function as plumbing is not to be relied on either. The artist (our Mutt) is, like most plumbers, nowhere to be found when you need him.

THE STRUGGLE

I ordered about twenty books and returned to G.12. Somebody was sitting in my seat. I informed him of the fact that
my twenty books would gradually be arriving in front of
him. He said he would pass them over the aisle to me, and
proceeded to do so, giggling about it every time. Why didn't
he just move? 'Artist stands back from product', I wrote half-
heartedly on a note-pad.

'Hello, Suze,' said a slightly foreign voice over my
shoulder. I looked up, and there was Johan Dirks, with whom
I had Jeopardized my Relationship with Jeremy once or twice
in 1982, until it had occurred to me to tell Johan that I didn't
want to Jeopardize my Relationship with Jeremy. It occurred
to me now that Johan was not strictly off limits, having
merely hankered after Franny, but not gone out with her. He
was also physically unlike Jeremy – large and heavy. He'd
written a Ph.D. in Leipzig on the sense of scale in art, and he
suddenly suited mine.

He had me over for Macaroni and Cheese, laboriously
created. We discussed going to bed together: Johan thought
we should, since we'd done so in the past – I thought we
shouldn't, for the same reason. The best solution in the end
seemed to be to run my hand up Johan's leg. He immediately
proposed we go to the bedroom, take off all our clothes, and
get into bed. This we did. We couldn't fuck, since neither of
us had any contraception, we agreed. But as soon as this was
settled, Johan began to seem a highly fuckable object to me,

86

an antidote to Jeremy before me in the flesh – his erection was pleasingly relentless, as erections go.

Afterwards, I felt embarrassed to have felt so passionate towards him. Irritated too at the prospect of the Morning-After Pill but all I needed at this stage in my life was a baby sired by Johan Dirks. He didn't really like sex, or women. Retreating into babyhood, he farted a lot and sucked my nipples until, much to his dismay, milk came out of them – he'd thought *he* was the only one emitting things. Just the fact that I was alive seemed to keep shocking him: not feminine of me. And all I wanted was some nice straightforward impersonal fucking – why all these kisses, farts, shocks?

I struggled to extricate myself from his flat without too long an aftermath. Just getting an aftermath established took some doing. He had idyllic plans for us: I should stay in bed while he got the sorbet or, if I must, I could get up but only put on a bathrobe. I took the easier course and stayed in bed. He returned with two tiny plastic containers of sorbet. Feigning a decent amount of post-coital tenderness, I let him share mine when he'd finished his.

When at last I sank with relief into my car, I regretted having wanted him, having fucked a guy who made me feel embarrassed about sex. And began to want him again. In fact, my impatience to see Johan Dirks grew and festered, bubbled and spat, all week, until I finally had to inform him that I was impatient. This of course perturbed him. He delayed meeting me. By the time we did converge, I had cooled down. He then accused me of having led him on, in fact of causing his nervous breakdown in 1982 with the same sort of behavior. After these preliminaries, and despite my continuing coldness, he tried to embrace me all evening, 1) because he fancied me and couldn't help it, and 2) because my refusals in the past had been merely a prelude to passionate hanky-panky.

I struggle to get Lily to the Primrose Hill playground: a special treat. First Lily takes off her shoes, so I unfold the pushchair and she re-enters it briefly. Then she agrees to put her shoes back on and we run around trees, kicking autumn leaves for a bit. Lily tries to seem cheerful. We run through leaves.

We reach the playground. Lily is duly swung. I look around and see that the world is grim. A three-legged Alsatian stands to attention outside the play area, and I'm just starting to wonder about the cause of its amputation when a red-faced man with a broken arm starts trying to get his little boy into a swing. I help them.

All the mothers are sitting together, either too cheery or too glum as they repeat to each other the phrase, 'There's never enough time in the day.' My eyes fall on an old woman sitting on a bench, with a white bandage on her nose.

I sat on a wall in the sun, discreetly eating Rich Tea Biscuits. Finally the yellow AA van appeared.

'Do you want to see my card?' I asked.

'Rather see the car. Worry about the car first, and the card later, eh? Talk to me! What's the matter with the old girl?'

'I think the battery's dead. My daughter may have left the lights on.'

'She as pretty as her mum? Okay, turn her over, let's hear what she's got to say for herself, eh?'

I turned the key and the car made no sound.

'Open the bonnet, will you, Love? When did you last have her maintained?'

How I hate the genderization of objects – I could never live in a country where that was going on all the time. Things you put things on are always female, like tables. Chaises-longues.

'January.'

'That's what you *say*, but the question is, do I believe you?' He smirked bewilderingly at me through the windscreen.

'Well, I had to have some work done then to pass the M.O.T.,' I ventured.

'Ah, but that doesn't mean she was *serviced*, does it? We all need that now and then, don't we, eh???' He scrutinized me closely, as if what he really wanted to say was: 'Honk if you had it last night.'

'This battery needs some distilled water,' he commented.

When he finally put the starter clamps on and got the car started, he conceded, 'Maybe you were right when you said you left the lights on. Are you shy, Love? Nice blond like you?! Just you seem very quiet.'

Of course I'm shy. So what?

'I've had a difficult morning, that's all,' I said. Who hasn't?

'Oh, what happened? Do you want to talk about it?' He peered through the open window with both elbows jutting in.

'Oh, no, I'd rather not think about it, thanks.'

'Oh well, I've had days like that too. But you shouldn't let it stop you smiling, Love. Don't like to see a pretty girl like you not smiling.'

I smiled for him.

'Well, I'm glad I could fix you up, especially as you've had such a rotten day. A lot of them are real old hags. I don't care about *them*. But I like fixing a car up for a pretty girl like you. You keep smiling now, Pussy-Cat!'

I was free! I drove around for half an hour to revive the battery, and to recover from the AA man. And was it AA policy to ignore the old bangers of old hags?

My little girl wants to wear pink shoes. She has lovely little grooves in baby places and dimples at the knee, and dirty feet. She's a person, and she wants to wear pink shoes.

> Cut out the shapes from Genoese, mask with
> hot apricot jelly, slightly warm your coloured and
> flavoured Marzipan, and roll out very thin. Pass a
> grooved rolling pin across to mark the lines, cut
> into strips with fluted cutter and cover the Genoese
> shapes. Fill in the centres with Fondant, jelly, etc.,
> and decorate.

I took Lily to Venice. I thought streets made of water might amuse, and anyway, *I* wanted to go. My hopes for the trip were raised by the handsome Italian train conductor who gave me the eye while punching my ticket. I left Lily asleep in the compartment with a friendly fellow traveller, and went to the loo. The ticket collector was still hanging around outside, waiting for me. He'd prepared his speech: 'You're beautiful.' I said that he was too. Then he pushed his tongue into my mouth and pushed me hard against the wall of the train in an imagined fuck. Then he pushed me into the loo and pushed me down, unzipped his trousers, and pushed my head down on his prick. I was feeling tired after a night on the train and rather enjoyed this manhandling. He snuck out of the loo first, to protect his job or his reputation. I crept out a minute later after washing my hands for some reason, feeling quite content.

Lily lost her hat in the canal as soon as we got out of the train station, and cried. Once she'd realized they were the main method of transportation, she refused to go on boats. I struggled up and down the steps of the little bridges, with the pushchair which I either hauled or carried. One wheel kept falling off all over Venice, Murano, Burano and Torcello.

We entered no churches, and no museums, until I made a

90

determined effort and got Lily to the Guggenheim collection. A storm broke out as we arrived, and Lily ran around the courtyard in the rain, taking her clothes off. When I scolded her mildly about this, she lay down on the marble floor, condensation rising almost visibly from her towards some Cubist *papiers collés,* and blocked a doorway. When she finally fell asleep in her pushchair, I wheeled her into Peggy Guggenheim's bedroom and went to the loo for a few moments' peace. Sixty seconds later, two or three of the bilingual, pre-parental, American Art History-major guards were knocking on the loo door, scared to death that the child had been abandoned to Peggy Guggenheim's care forever.

I trudged, Lily complained, my money ran low, and meanwhile, the heat and the handsome men continued to make me feel randy. Even the male pigeons I found sexy, stalking females in St Mark's Square, with their necks all puffed out, though I noted that they were easily swayed from this quest whenever Lily threw them corn. I was approached in restaurants every night by their human equivalent, loose men who were strangely indifferent to my reaction to them – they bounced back or took off, with the same blank expression either way. They all had teddy-bear names, like Nildo, Naldo, Bepe and Pepe.

A restaurant-owner called Mimmo gave Lily some nice noodles and freshly squeezed orange juice, for which I was grateful, since all the other restaurants were shutting. He placed a tiny TV in front of her which she happily watched, undeterred by the language barrier. I relaxed. I rather liked . Mimmo – he knew too little English to put me off. We started kissing. It was not bad. At least he showed determination.

He wanted me to come back and see his flat. I explained that this was out of the question with Lily around. He said, just come see it so I would know where it was and could then come to lunch some time. It made no sense to me. But Lily wanted to go, so we went. We saw his raggedy carpet and his unmade bed and the bits of cotton wool on the floor. I had never thought before about the fact that they had cotton wool in Italy too.

He started to straighten it all up a bit. I started to go. I called Lily, but she was sitting down on a little stool in Mimmo's bedroom, too tired to move. I was heading back to go pick her up, when Mimmo grabbed me and pressed me against the wall, kissing my closed lips. I suddenly realized that he felt he had a right to do anything to me, because I'd had the audacity to go to his flat. When I tried to push at the arms holding me, he pushed harder. I made myself cold and stiff, saying, 'Stop. Stop it,' again and again. I wondered how I could explain even to good friends, much less the police, that I hadn't intended to fuck this person. He suddenly relented – he must have realized it would be quite hard to rape me, and perhaps he even grasped the fact that it would be no fun.

I wandered, trembling and furious, back to his bedroom to collect my whimpering child. Mimmo escorted us back to our *pensione*, pretending that nothing had happened. He asked me to come for lunch the next day. I was too scared to say anything.

I could no longer cope with Venice. I kept crying. I wept almost continually on the train home. Lily offered me sweets, and waited for me to recover. Back in London, she still wants pink shoes. I keep seeing Mimmo's face everywhere.

Don't Say YES When You Want To Say NO
Yes, now you too can break from a self-limiting way of life, as countless graduates of Assertiveness Training can testify, launching yourself on a life-changing program which is easier than you think!

SATELLITE CONNECTION

'Each jealous of the other, as the stung
Are of the adder.'

Write letters – that's what sisters who are close are supposed to do, even daily to Australia. Franny phoned, from Vermont. She phoned to tell me she'd broken her self-imposed chastity and was having a wild affair with ironically a British art student. She claimed she'd never had a real orgasm until now. She was overwhelmed by sex and sensuality for the first time in her life.

'What do all your feminist chums make of this?' I asked, at a loss for anything better to say.

'I guess I'm looking pretty good these days, you know? I'm pretty thin – I was so poor recently. The bank wouldn't let me have any money, so I was living literally on yoghurts [Boysenberry]. And then this beautiful guy asks me out to dinner. I couldn't refuse, I was too hungry! So he bought me a huge steak, and after I'd eaten it all, well, he turned out to be this incredible lover.'

'It strikes me I've heard that line somewhere before.'

'Aw, Suzy. You've got to meet him. When are you going to come visit me anyway?'

It was the first I'd heard of her wish for me to visit.

'When you pay me the fifty bucks you owe me for meeting a man within five years!'

Franchipan Fancies
Fill the boat with franchipan mixing, and then
pipe lines across the sweet paste which has
been previously thinned with water to piping
consistency. When baked, wash over with hot
apricot jelly.

The Private View was in full swing when I got there, a
rowdy gathering tucked inconspicuously away in the middle
of Cork Street. Nothing like some of the ones I go to, where
the dealer looks you up and down to see if you've only come
for the booze. I followed a large edifice of a man into the
gallery, but somehow got ahead of him on our way to the
champagne. A man in an ornate tuxedo was pouring eagerly.
Most of the people there looked like they'd never done
anything else in their lives except go to Cork Street openings,
and never done anything else with their hands but gesture
listlessly towards paintings. Yet none of them seemed to be
talking about art (the last resort of the uninitiated). I noticed
several empty wine-glasses atop a small glass case in which a
Gaudier-Brzeska sculpture sat – his every work has been
treasured since his early death.

I was not in a good mood. I wanted to down some
champagne and see a few pictures. The pictures, from what I
could tell, were pink; the champagne was normal. My eyes
rested in the end on the abundance of red hair working its
way down the back of the girl ahead of me. Not bright tangy
red, but like rust dampened with grey or green. It was hard
to believe that such a color could last the length of the hair,
and I set to wondering what progress had been made in
producing children from two women. Genetically, wouldn't
this serve nature's purposes perfectly well? Of course,
genetically, red hair poses some problems. But maybe it was
dyed, anyway. Chris Taft's red hair was flashing at me

through pine trees in my mind when I was startled out of my reverie by Alan Fry, who ran *D.K. Magazine* (short for 'Detailed Knowledge'), for which I'd written the occasional exhibition review.

'What do you make of them?' he asked me, flicking his five-o'clock be-shadowed chin towards the pink paintings.

I mouthed on about idiosyncratic lines, the flatness of the picture plane, and indeterminacy, in an evidently satisfactory manner, for he asked me out to dinner.

> When a scientist is working on experiments he very often needs a container to hold liquids. This piece of apparatus is called a beaker. A beaker has a lip for easy pouring.

We walked to a pasta place Alan Fry knew. He stopped so abruptly outside it, I sprinkled every single ingredient of my bag on to the pavement. He waited, a little impatiently I thought, while I recovered myself.

'Where do you come from?' he asked, when we were finally seated. 'I imagine you from Minnesota: barn-dances and apple pie.'

I was not particularly flattered – do people from Minnesota drop a lot of handbags?

'No, not Minnesota,' I said mysteriously. 'My mother went there once – a lot of snow.' Flucked again. Alan Fry was fascinated by Americana, the quainter the better: his speech was littered with semi-assimilated slang, and the occasional attempt at an American accent. And I'd failed him: I was not from Minnesota.

'How long have you lived here anyway?' he asked somewhat suspiciously.

'Oh, sixteen years.'

'You haven't lost your accent.'

'No, I decided not to.'

'You sound likè you just got off the boat! You're not thinking of going back in the near future, are you?'

'Well, I *was* thinking of going back for a visit,' I said quickly. 'My sister's in Vermont until the end of this year and I'd kind of like to–'

'Oh, Fran! How's she doing? It really breaks me up she hasn't been working for us lately.'

He was presented with penne, I with gnocchi, which always make my heart sink.

'She's okay,' I said.

'Well, if you're going over anyway, you fancy a trip to the Big Apple? Do you know Manhattan?'

'Well, a bit. Why?' I asked, flustered but hopeful.

'Okay. Call ol' Fran and tell her you're coming,' he said masterfully. 'We need an article on the New Wave, all these fat-assed East Village guys that're taking over the art market. You're perfect for the job: you're *American*.' He pronounced the word with relish. 'Maybe you can figure them out.'

'I don't know much–'

'Nobody knows anything about them over here! Though you must've heard of Ken Derring?'

I nodded.

'And who else? Oh, there's this guy called Gorot. He's French, and black – or at least one or the other. He's been collaborating with Warhol.'

'Hasn't everyone?' I piped up adroitly, I thought.

'Ha! And there's Al Pole, and Rob Dole, and Burlo . . .'

I hadn't heard of a single one of them. I bluffed it out by eating gnocchi. Alan Fry talked on, about discourses, and new galleries, and graffiti, and Schlamowitz, and discourses. I tried to follow him, and wished I was anywhere else, except that he was rather good-looking. In fact, by the time we'd finished eating, I found I'd enthusiastically agreed to the proposal that I go to New York for a few weeks, interview the New Wave, and report back to *D.K.* on the subject.

Alan Fry wasn't going to pay me much, since I was going anyway, but he'd pay for a few meals in New York, he said. He also didn't seem to want to take me to bed, so we parted company on Albermarle Street, a name that has always seemed to me to imitate in sound the contours of a cunt. I didn't bother saying this to Alan Fry, though – I'd impressed him enough for one evening.

I felt disgruntled all the way home on the bus, and when I got home, I looked Alan Fry up in the phone-book and peered at his Kensington address and phone-number, wondering if I should call him up and tell him I fancied him. But I was scared of losing what little work *D.K.* gave me, and especially the New York job. I called Franny instead. She seemed a bit peeved I'd been asked to do a whole article for *D.K.*, and asked dubiously what I was planning to do with Lily if I came.

'Jeremy can probably take her – he's not working at the moment. But where will I stay in New York? Do you know anybody– Oh, I know! I could stay with Melanie.'

'Do you still keep in touch with that dumbo?' Franny asked.

'How's it going with John?' I asked.

'Oh, scrumptious. Literally: he's always buying me nice things to eat!' She giggled.

'Oh.'

'Hey, you could do me a favor, Suzy. Would you help me move all my stuff? I've decided to come back at Christmas instead of in the summer.'

'Oh.' (Franny back in town.)

'John is going back at Christmas, you see.'

'Oh.' (Franny-plus-boyfriend back in town.)

CONTINENTAL DRIFT

Jeremy had found himself a flat; it had only taken him about nine months. We arranged things so that he could take care of Lily in the house, and then move out on my return. I moved everything out of my Pimlico place to confirm this plan.

I arrived in New York in late November. Melanie's husband, just back from a three-month stay in Java researching a seventeenth-century sculptor for his Ph.D., remained in his Study most of the time, laughing to himself. Melanie intermittently urged him to go to a psychiatrist, and made him cookies, which he ate in huge quantities and then berated her for making him fat. He was considering divorce – not a bad idea I thought, under the circumstances, though part of me envied them. After all, they still had sex, and cookies.

> What you are about to read
> is stranger than fiction
> and concerns two ordinary
> looking objects.

'Guess who I saw in a book-shop the other day,' Melanie said, as we sat in her kitchen eating Molasses Bread soon after my arrival.

'Who?' I asked, not expecting to have ever heard of whoever it was.

'Christopher Taft!'

'Are you kidding?!'

'No. And you should see him! He's a banker.'

'Are you kidding?'

'He's living in Brooklyn Heights.'

'What, is that expensive or something?'

'Oh, very chi–chi!'

'Huh!'

I ruminated over this information while I plodded around the East Village the next day, looking hesitantly into dumpy little galleries. I bought a cheap tape-recorder on 47th Street and with it interviewed all the wrong people.

> *I love you, and you're not just a*
> *sex object to me, though I was real*
> *turned on in the chapel when my*
> *hand was on your breast and we were*
> *kissing, I don't want to use the word*
> *tit because it sounds slummy.*

I wandered down Avenues A, B and C, past junkies sleeping in the snow, and thought of my own emptiness. I thought how nobody had loved me since Christopher Taft. I thought how little I liked neo-graffiti artists and New York in the cold. When I got back to Melanie's apartment, I phoned Franny and asked her to get me Chris' number in Brooklyn Heights. Franny reluctantly phoned Kate Taft in Oklahoma, who turned out to be recovering from a debilitating disease she'd caught in Africa five years before – the disease had a seven-year span. Inbetween bouts, Kate was working in a dog kennel. Nonetheless, she managed to give Franny Chris' number. Three or four days later Franny called me with it. I'd already looked him up in the phone-book by then and called him.

'Suzy Schwarz!' he said. His voice affected me as it always had. Terrible that I'd been without him for so long.

'How are you?' I asked.

'Oh, fine. How àre you?'

'Okay. Uh, Melanie tells me you're in banking now?'

'Yeah. What are *you* doing? What are you doing in New York?!'

'Oh, well, I'm trying to write an article about the new East Village art scene. Hey, Chris, um, did you ever get a letter a few years ago by any chance, I mean, a letter from *me*? It's just, you never replied.' I held the receiver away from my wavering voice.

'A letter? No, I haven't had a letter from you as far as I know for about fifteen years!'

'Oh, well, maybe I forgot to send it.' (Saved.)

'Maybe my parents didn't forward it. Hey, you know, I have a small Ken Derring picture!'

'Really? What of?' (His *parents* had opened it!?)

'Oh, a barking dog and a crawling baby,' he said.

'Well, I must admit I've seen a lot of those! Though not small ones.'

It was all very polite. We arranged to meet at the Yale Club that Thursday. Meanwhile, I pursued my study of New York culture. I had a huge breakfast with a vague friend of Franny's who was into mysticism and meditation herself but claimed to know a lot about the current scene.

'They have no particular aims, except painting to make money. Start a competition for a picture called "Shit in a Trash-can" and they'll all paint pictures for it,' she told me. 'There's a whole bunch of them that only paint pictures of TV aerials, pylons, and telegraph poles.'

The galleries were called things like Scum, Hard-On, Brackish Water, 52-J, and Fun, and everybody was indeed talking about Warhol all over again. He was publishing a gigantic magazine that I made good use of one day, to keep the snow off practically my whole body. Tickle-Two-Tums, a subway graffiti artist, had even painted a series of Brillo-pad boxes across several trains. I decided to write the article about appropriation: people running around stealing stuff and calling themselves artists. My theme was really the absent artist, as per usual.

Thursday arrived. I dressed casually – in several layers of my sexiest clothing – and went to the Yale Club, near Grand Central Station. I walked in at the appointed hour and sat down in the foyer (which was as far as unaccompanied women could go). Across from me sat three old men, reading their papers. One got up and approached me. I still didn't recognize him.

'You look just the same,' he said.

It was Chris Taft. He had allowed his red hair to thin and turn brown.

We tried to find somewhere else to have tea, but in the end gave up and just sat in the lounge of some hotel. He asked me why I'd wanted to see him.

> Put a blackboard on the ground
> and get someone to sit on it.
> Try to push the blackboard along.
> Will it move?
>
> Put some soapy water on your
> hand. Now try to open the door.

MY NEW FOUND LAND

You will need an empty shoe polish tin.

Telephones are an important feature of New York life, and one with which New Yorkers seem strangely comfortable. Everyone has an answering machine so with any luck you never have to talk to the real person, but there's also an intimidating service that allows you to talk to two real people at the same time. You're talking to Party No 1 and you hear a distinctive click. So you say, wait a sec, somebody else on the line, and you press down the receiver button and thereby get hold of Party No 2. After discovering who Party No 2 happens to be, you're then faced with this awful dilemma, a nightmare for those of us without social aplomb: you decide who you'd rather speak to and tell the other one you'll call them back. People pay the phone company for this privilege.

'Just a sec, Franny, there's someone else on the line,' I said with some satisfaction, and switched into the air waves of an artist I'd been referred to by somebody or other. I then clicked back to Franny and told her I'd call her later.

'Well, when would you like to come?' the artist asked me.

'Tomorrow, if that's convenient for you. I don't have much time to spend in New York – I'm supposed to be in Vermont.'

'Fine. Third floor.'

'Oh, but what time, please?'

'Any time.'

I set out the next day without much enthusiasm. Not more with-it artists. At the shop belonging to Scum Gallery, I decided to check out the bargains I'd heard that the gallery's artists provided specially for the shop. The small plastic decapitated babies were cheap. In fact their only real competition for rock-bottom prices were some cone-shaped objects you were supposed to wear on your nose in order to gouge people's eyes out.

I was pretty tired of New York, too tired to try to figure out exactly where he lived, so I took a taxi. I was dreading the sight of more terrible paintings, the need to be polite and to think up intelligent questions. The taxi-driver was clearly psychotic. He weaved through Houston Street as if he were trying to evade a barrage of snipers' bullets. I was almost in tears when he finally let me out still alive, into the beginnings of a snowstorm.

No one answered the front door of Jim Carlucci's apartment building. The third-floor windows were too high for me to throw a stone, if I could have found one. I was beginning to think about taking another taxi straight back to Melanie's, when a scruffy guy came up and went into the building. I squeezed through the door with him just in time. He snorted. I asked him if this was where Jim Carlucci lived. He said nothing and disappeared surprisingly fast up the stairs. I went up two flights and knocked on the first door I came to. A beautiful man, somewhat pudgy with rumpled yellow hair, answered it.

'Sorry to bother you, but I'm looking for Jim Carlucci.'
'That's me. Come on in. Want some tea?'
I asked him a lot of dumb questions, receiving replies like 'Nope' and 'Yep' and 'So what?' I stirred honey into my tea feeling increasingly hopeless, until he brought out a joint and showed me his paintings. No collage, no violence. As if nature were welcome here in the heart, or ass, of Manhattan, his pictures were of big trees, striving hard for the light of the

orange or yellow sky behind them, filling the canvas with a mass of botanical groins.

'Pretty sexy,' I suggested.

'Really? I've forgotten sex. That's why I'm making such a play for you.'

I cheered up.

He went off to have a shower. I sat there, feeling hunger of various kinds. For a long time there was the sound of water running. Finally, I went into the little bathroom that was covered in tiny white tiles. He was there, his naked body behind the textured glass, as if preserved in ice for me.

I slid the glass door to the side, put my hand on his wet, warm chest, and kissed him. He held my head to his. I stepped into the shower, still wearing my East Side interviewing garb: I had to put my legs around him.

The water got too hot. He turned it down. I felt it running all over me and changing temperature, as he dragged my sticky clothes off. Before, behind, between, above, below.

Two figures lit by a little light, six hours difference, now far back in the past. My America. I begged him to fuck me and fuck me and fuck me, and as he did so later on the bed, he said that he was made for me, which I considered corny, but true.

Sacrum
Ileum
Ischium
Pubis

ASSEMBLE WITH FOUR LONG SCREWS
FIX BOTTOM AND MIDDLE FITTINGS
TO LEGS ON THE OPEN SIDE

With Jim's help, I got a little farther with the New Wave, about which he had his reservations: 'It's like a lot of bored Central Park Plaza brats that want to get into the Bad, when we're here struggling like hell to get *rid* of it. We don't find any romance in junk. And when *they* move in, we can't afford to live here anymore. It's all part of the Redevelopment program.' I stopped going out and just taped Jim.

But always the trip to Vermont loomed. Franny was getting impatient – I was supposed to be helping her pack and here I was, fucking around in New York. On my last possible night, Jim took me to *The Barber of Seville*, his favorite opera. I found it tender, and cried. It seemed to be about imprisonment.

I said I'd take him out for Japanese food afterwards, but first we went for a drink at an artsy bar where we met an old geezer who seemed to be an artist, gay, and interested in Jim. They talked and talked. I drank Manhattans. I tried at first to participate but the other guy ignored me. Jim seemed enthralled by him. In the end, he invited the guy to come eat Japanese food with us. I was amazed – was I supposed to pay for this guy to hog sushi *and* Jim all evening?

I could hardly bring myself to speak when we parted from the creep, who didn't even want to come anyway. I was so angry, speechless with rage. When we got to the restaurant, Jim asked me if I was annoyed with him, and urged me to spit it out if I was. I finally admitted I was and he got all excited! He was very pleased. He said I'd been treating him so nicely all the time, he hadn't known what to make of it, but now he knew he loved me. I had a feeling this decision was somewhat influenced by the dress I was wearing, a clingy black number, but I too felt strangely energized by this near breakdown of relations. We stared lustfully at each other over raised wooden platforms of raw fish until the restaurant presented us each with a Japanese mug – it was their third anniversary – and sent us home.

Jim lay across my legs that night, now and then looking into my eyes as he mashed his face into my cunt. He decided to come with me to Vermont. I instantly began to fear that Franny would either dislike him, or somehow manage to take him from me. He told me nothing bad would happen.

We rented a car the next day and headed North, stopping whenever our clandestine caresses became urgent.

Outline

I. Beginning
   A *Main characters*
      1 Melanie
      2 Lynn
      3 Patty
      4 Bus-driver
      5 Mrs Turpin
      6 Me
   B *Setting*
      1 Time: 2.30, Tuesday, February
      2 Place: highway in Chicago, Ill.
   C *Situation*: a bus accident

II Middle: Events – concert, Horse game, bus
            turning, going over snow . . .
III End
   A *Final event*: bumping into tree
   B *Summary statement*: results – Lynn's broken
      leg, bus-driver's cut, my scratches,
      Melanie's dizziness, Patty's O.K.ness

Franny and I started arguing as soon as I arrived. According to her, Jim and I were three hours late. According to my calculations, we were only about an hour and a half late. She said it didn't matter, she'd just been worried about us. She took a look at Jim and raised her eyebrows at me in an appreciative manner. She became rather flirtatious, in fact. We went out to supper at a fancy place where the wait-person had to recite a pretentious menu she'd learnt by heart: it's supposed to be an added luxury for the customer not to have to learn how to read. We made her repeat a lot of it.

Franny gave up her bed to us that night. I had a shower and caught Franny's eye on the way back from the bathroom. She whispered, '*He's* nice! But I don't think he likes me.' Then she told me that John had been treating her badly: he had another girlfriend in England he was going back to.

I retreated to Franny's bedroom feeling guilty about having my nice man waiting for me in there. Jim was sitting on the floor, reading a newspaper. What will future cultural historians think when they find out how much of everyone's time in the twentieth century was spent on newspaper perusal? To spare them a little bewilderment, I put a bare clean leg over Jim's shoulder and sank myself down on him like a Borneo woman making a pass. He pulled me down onto the floor then, keeping my legs open with his arm.

The next day, after bagels for breakfast (Franny's favorite) and orange juice (ditto), we began packing the car and arguing. Franny's computer inside its padding inside its box inside its case inside its cardboard box underneath a blanket couldn't have anything put on top of it, not even a clothes-hanger. Four large suitcases, a radio, a box of books, a large shaggy lampshade with protruding wires and the computer accessories all had to be squidged in elsewhere, meaning that we didn't even have room to take Jim as far as the train station. He took a taxi.

We smoked a last joint together.

'I'll miss you,' I said. 'Immensely.'

'You shouldn't miss me immensely – you should be having a swinging social life. Hey, but write to me. I love you.' It reminded me of similarly hopeless statements, made under similar pressure from the Atlantic, fifteen years earlier.

He urged autonomy on me, when I hadn't yet satisfied the pubescent longing to unbutton and reveal all those soft sad corners. I felt around for my shell as I watched him go, and climbed back into it.

Leaving behind forever the beautiful miniature piano Franny had bought for Lily (it didn't fit in the car), two grumpy women set off on the long haul to Boston's Logan airport. We argued about the choice of route: the ridiculousness of mine, the nonexistence of Franny's. We argued about Franny's directions: whether she'd given them, whether I'd misheard them. We headed in the direction of Nova Scotia.

The rest of the time we argued about personal, sexual and emotional matters. To rid myself of a vivid image of cutting Franny up into thick slices that looked like white bread, I turned my thoughts to the sex of the previous night (it works well in the dentist's chair too). As if sensing my mental desertion of the car scene, Franny suddenly said, 'Not very bright, is he?'

I hoped she didn't mean Jim. 'Who you talking about?'

'Jim! Who'd you think? Terribly chauvinistic too. Must be the Italian in him. How do you *find* people like that, Suzy?' she enquired.

'I thought you liked him!'

'I did, until all that stuff at the restaurant about waitresses.'

I wasn't sure what the hell she meant, all I knew was she'd wrecked it for me.

I dumped Franny and her belongings at the TWA check-in desk and drove several times around Logan airport looking for the right place to return the car. Then I waited in a long line and when I finally got to the front of it, had to pay extra money. But the Hertz wait, though itself distressing, spared me any more of Franny's company until the last minute before we had to go to the passenger lounge, at which point I spent a good deal of time in the loo, feeling out a new continent of despair.

Though she'd ˙expressed doubts about returning to England, Franny seemed elated on the plane, and drank champagne. I nursed a cut I'd gotten from her lampshade.

Keep your wound as clean and dry as possible.

At Heathrow, we rented yet another car that was too small. This time Franny drove, terrifyingly carefully (she'd just learned how). She frowned when I snagged her lampshade on the car-door getting it out, but once I'd carried all her possessions into her flat, and sat around while she sorted some of them out, she took me to a Greek restaurant where people broke a lot of plates on purpose and danced in a long silly line around our table.

'Strike flat the thick rotundity
of the world!'

FOUND OBJECTS

Another individual term. Suzy doesn't participate in the life of the school at all.

It was very nice to see Lily again. I'd missed her. Immensely. Her little hands were dear to hold. She drew pictures of smiling butterflies and said, 'Suzy, do you hope I'm happy?'

I said, 'Yes. Are you?'

'Yes. I'm happy like these butterflies'

I resumed my jaunts to the laundromat, Jeremy having removed his washing-machine in a moving-van. Meanwhile, the ill-informed Irving continued to forward all of Jeremy's junk mail to my house.

Daddy came up to London to see me settled again. He asked if he could see my thesis too, so I had to give him a thirty-page essay I'd done some time before – a collage of different interpretations of collage. He was astounded by the messiness of my house. Jeremy had made no attempt to clean it up before he left (taking care of Lily was as much as I could ask of him), while I had been busy on the East Side article since my return, and had made no headway as yet with the many junk-rooms Jeremy had created.

> 'On a recent trip to New York, I decided to check out the newly rich East Village, where eighty new galleries have opened up within the last five years, selling the semi-subversive found objects of the latest found artists.'

I could not bring myself to write to Jim. He phoned and I said everything was all right, but in fact my mind had become pre-occupied with the notion that I might have caught AIDS from him – I'd decided he was bisexual. Franny meanwhile re-established amorous relations with John.

I sit looking at my typewriter and out of the window through the crack in the curtain I've allowed myself, and think about the guy on the French train. He claimed he was a policeman. He'd been on a case in Cannes, where his main discovery seemed to have been that tomatoes were overpriced. I'd been in Nice looking at Matisse in connection with my MA at the Courtauld. I had to talk to him for hours in my shaky French. I went to the loo while the couchette-man was making up our beds. As I brushed my teeth, I decided that it would be all right if the policeman made a pass, it might even be interesting. The door to our compartment was locked when I got back – an excuse, it seemed, for him to lock it again after I came in. I hauled myself onto the top bunk. The policeman explained to me the mechanics of my reading-light, and then got into the bunk below. I read happily enough for a few minutes, before he stood up and declared he wanted to kiss me (vb. *embracer*).

'*Vraiment?*' was my suave reply.

The guy was passionate, with a big tongue and a big prick which he soon rammed into me. On that top bunk he made me come. People hammered on the door to be allowed to go to bed.

Dismal metro journey together the next day. I didn't want to spoil the encounter by repeating it, so I duly informed him that there was *un autr'homme*. Dismal solitude of my dismal hotel room. Dismal *autr'homme*.

I suddenly realize that I am extremely sick of seeing the perfectly formed ballerina every time I go to the loo, and of being reminded what kind of whisky she drinks after a night spent tripping across the boards, or whatever they do. I turn the magazine over as I sit down on the loo, and find inside a review by someone I once remotely fancied. Waves of abdominal pain course through me as I read his deliberations on Hiroshima, deliberately full of alliterative p's.

'This is shit!' I exclaim.

I eventually return to my desk and locate the apples – red American ones, which I was embarrassed to buy for fear of seeming patriotic. They look better than they taste. It occurs to me that if I take Lily to school and then go to the DHSS office and receive my numbered ticket in the queue, I could then go to the VD clinic and have my pre-AIDS-test-counselling and my AIDS test and my AIDS-test-debriefing, and probably be back in the DHSS office before my number was called, so that with any luck both errands could be accomplished within Lily's six-hour school-day.

I've attempted to avoid work all day. I now tidy my desk, my books, and my records (I manage to refrain from arranging my ten cassette-tapes in alphabetical order as well – I only play Rossini these days anyway), I load the new washing-machine Daddy bought me when he saw my plight, with whites, I make tea, I check the TV programs for the coming week, I rearrange the papers on my desk and then sit down at it to write:

1
22
333
4444
55555
666666
7777777
666666
55555
4444
333
22
1

etcetera, etcetera, àll the way down the page in an attempt at a shapely sideways mountain-range, sometimes including 8's and 9's. I watch this sheet of paper float to the floor as I grab another on which to draw an iris that soon turns into an infinite pile of bananas. I trim my fingernails. I eat crackers. I hoover up the debris from both activities, and then veer out of the room and hoover the stairs. I stare at the African bark painting above my desk for some minutes, and then have a bath – I need one.

I dry my hair with the blow-dryer, and administer rouge to my cheeks in the manner prescribed by a make-up salesgirl at Boots five years ago (after I gave up my boycott of the whole Boots chain). The time nears for my release from work. I put Figaro on again.

> 'Tutti mi chiedono.
> Tutti mi vogliono.
> Donne, ragazzi,
> Vecchi, fanciulle.'

Daddy returned my essay to me with so many corrections all over it that I couldn't bring myself to look at it, except for the bits where he'd written, 'good'. I didn't want to look at Daddy either – he didn't seem very well.

It was the year they took the statue of Eros out of Piccadilly, to make room for more cars.

> . . . besides the instinct to preserve living substance and to join it into ever larger units, there must exist another contrary instinct seeking to dissolve those units and to bring them back to their primaeval, inorganic state . . .

Such bullshit. Death is the least natural thing in the world, the opposite of nature.

I was cold, so I had a cup of tea. Then I was too hot. I suddenly felt ready to write to British Telecom.

Dear Sir or Madam,

It may, or of course it may not, interest you to know that my telephone has been on the blink for two weeks. During this period I have had recourse to the public telephones in my area, which are also on the blink. I have been passed around amongst BT employees to little avail. On Monday morning I spoke to an insolent young man. I didn't dare call again on Tuesday, for fear of annoying him, but was relieved on Wednesday to get hold of an apparently different man. He was unfortunately unable to tell me anything but that the engineers had reportedly fixed my phone on Tuesday.

I took this opportunity to declare that my telephonic apparatus was nonetheless not functioning, and that I needed it to function. He said he'd give my telephone priority. On Thursday, I got a woman who refused to give it priority. On Friday, the insolent guy was back, pretending to be the nice guy. Detecting the necessary note of distress in my voice, he suggested I call Customer Services. Customer Services provided a sympathetic personage who commiserated but could only promise to beg on my behalf, which did not sound promising. Nonetheless, I fell deeply in love. To this man, I was at last able to confide in full my urgent need for a telephone (see below). Though it was clear from his pleasant tone that the gentleman could have no power within the company, I felt somewhat better after this exchange.

Perhaps I should explain. I have recently spent a great deal of time and money replying to personal ads and was expecting to hear from people this week. I (irrationally, I know) regard my telephone's utter silence as a massive rejection of my epistolary advances (photos

*included), and have taken to drink as a result, never
mind the cookies. Being forlorn is quite expensive on my
meager income (am I still renting my defunct telephone
all this time, by the by?).*

*When I rang British Telecom today, the right tone of
voice was once again detected, thus qualifying me for
another referral to Customer Services. The Servant I
then spoke to offered me something I now recognize as
really special: the number of someone with a name! A
name, o! frabjous day kaloo kalay. 'Mrs Kennedy' – I
shall treasure it, it's branded on my heart in a mass of
microscopic colored wires, yes, YES! I was told to speak
to Mrs Kennedy.*

*I imagine her as a strong, maternal type, able to battle
her full-bosomed way through red tape, red hands, in fact
any birthing difficulty telephone technicians or clients
may be caught encountering. Hired like Aunt Jemima,
to give the operation a bit of class and keep us suckers
busy while some External Engineer is stubbing his cig
out on the crucial wire connecting one's home with the
outside world. I have a weakness for maternal substitutes,
possibly explained by certain aspects of my upbringing,
several aspects in fact, come to think of it, so I was rather
looking forward to calling up your Mrs Kennedy for a
little chat, but thought I should wait a bit, save it up for
later: I'd been talking to BT all morning as it was.*

*I went straight home therefore and got the squids out of
the fridge. I wrestled with their horny assholes and
globular eyes and sacs of orange eggs. One had neither
eggs nor liver. I steamed what seemed theoretically
edible, but my neighbor called me out into the backyard
during this delicate process, and it seemed necessary to
peer, and expound, back at her – she has a lot of flower
pots that my cat shits in, so I have to be nice. As soon as
I could, I returned to the squids which were by then*

rubbery, except for the liverish bits, which were
disintegrating.

   I turned on the radio, tuning into my favorite
program. There was a woman on it who hadn't had sex
with her husband for fifteen years. He was impotent.
The two doctors in the studio decided this was all her
fault, for having wanted sex in the first place.
Undaunted, the woman mentioned that every six weeks
or so, she still wants it. The doctors cautioned her,
saying that it was the Relationship, not Sex, that was
important, especially as one gets older. What do they
know?

   I turned on the TV after this to watch an old film
featuring Norma Shearer and What's-his-name.
I couldn't face going out to phone Mrs Kennedy at this
point. People were falling in love all over the place. I
cried a bit when What's-his-name's bride gets shot on the
altar by the jilted lover. In the middle of all this, my
phone rang. It was the External Engineer. Giving me
no explanation for the weeks of telephonic torment, he
told me my phone was now working, and thus wrecked
my plans of calling Mrs Kennedy to complain.

   You have substituted one source of frustration for
another, Sir, or Madam, and ought to be ashamed.

   Yours (since you have a monopoly),
      Susan Schwarz

ARTIFICIAL FLAVORS

Goldberg's a private in the army. His mother dies, and his superior officers don't know how to break the news to him. His sergeant volunteers to do it. He calls the whole platoon out, makes them all stand at attention, and then says,

'All those with mothers still living, step forward!'

They all step forward.

'Not so fast, Goldberg!'

My father was the great joke-teller, and now he was having trouble talking and moving his head. I went to see his doctor. I'd assumed he wasn't taking my father's ailments seriously, when in fact they were by now affecting his ability to drive.

The doctor told me my father was dying.

Goldstein's two partners are appalled when Goldstein kicks the bucket during the course of the working day. After some discussion, the more tactful of the two goes to tell Goldstein's wife. Knocks on the door. Woman answers.

'Widow Goldstein?'

'I'm *Mrs* Goldstein. I'm not a widow!'

'Wanna bet?'

When his doctor finally called my father into the surgery to tell him, Daddy was furious with me for having known and done nothing. I hadn't even looked the disease up in the *Encyclopaedia Britannica*, I now realized. He did.

He telephoned me when he'd had the diagnosis confirmed by a neurologist. I didn't know what to say.

'When I told Fran, she cried,' he said reproachfully.

> 'We'll no more meet, no more see one another;
> But yet thou art my flesh, my blood, my daughter;
> Or rather a disease that's in my flesh,
> Which I must needs call mine: thou art a boil,
> A plague-sore, an embossed carbuncle,
> In my corrupted blood.'

I sit in the car, in the quiet square, facing the building in question. I get out and lock the door. I walk into the foyer and ask where to go. Through some swinging doors I find Franny and Daddy, the one solicitous, the other merely glum. Franny has on a violently violet sweater and snazzy black-and-white shoes. Daddy's wearing his neck-brace. I sit down. We wait.

We're ushered in. We all sit in a row in front of the doctor. He confirms that Daddy is dying. Daddy has a series of queries he's prepared for this moment. He has the neurologist write down his answers in the spaces provided. Franny and I ask a few questions too. We all troop out. We have had the Second Opinion.

> What will a neurologist do once the
> disease is identified?

> *Try to manage the progress of the disease.*

We go to Bloom's afterwards to eat kosher food. Slabs of salt beef and two long pale pickles (indivisible between three) await us. I park the car much too far away. Using up what muscles Daddy's got left, we start walking up Brick Lane. Franny remembers something she's left in my car and goes back for it. Daddy keeps turning around to look for her, all the way to Bloom's: she'd always had a tendency to get lost.

WIND

What's the Matter With the American Stomach?

Evidently something is the matter. We
are known the world over as a nation of
dyspeptics. 'Uncle Sam' as pictured, has
a lean and hungry look. The United
States has half as many doctors as all the
rest of the world.

The average American is anemic. He
has only four-fifths as much blood as he
should have – only four-fifths alive.
Millions are less than half alive.

As my father wasted away, I ate. Once I knew he was dying,
I ate and ate for two weeks solid, until I felt as solid as he'd
once seemed. I ate so much my throat felt bruised and my
body ached. My shoulders, lower back, the skin across my
ribs, were all sore in different ways. I could feel the fat on my
shins wiggle as I walked. I didn't want to talk to anyone in
case they sensed how pathetic I was, even without clear
indications like breadcrumbs on my cheeks.

I didn't want to talk about the situation. Holding my
tender breasts and stomach in my arms like a bundle of
babies, I made a world for myself which only I inhabited. I
dreaded the telephone, I wanted to hibernate. In my private
world I ate all day and stayed up late at night merely in order
to eat some more. I had no use for friends – my life centred

around the fridge, the bread-box and a few of the kitchen cupboards.

I dreaded having a bath, I did not want to think about my mortal frame. I didn't touch myself more than I could help. And I had no time within all this indigestible inner turmoil to consider my father much at all. I told myself I was such a mess I could not concern myself with anyone. I wanted to owe no one anything. I kept thinking, with some sadness, but also some satisfaction, nobody knows what I'm up to.

The newspaper headlines lining the length of the long carriage spoke of the Big Chill, just as one summer they'd dwelt on the 'Phew!' hot spells. But it was already over: the snow was slushy. Unbelievable anyway that there could ever be snow in Slough.

All I wanted was to get off that train, buy some bread, get into the loo in our house in Oxford, and eat it. I didn't want love or sex or beauty – the thing I wanted to get my hands on was bread. Wearing the shapeless coat I'd recently bought to hide inside, I hobbled down the streets of Oxford like an old woman, bent by my shameful quest, and the slipperiness of my boots. Oxford was cold and dark, as per usual.

I passed trees knocked down by the recent winds. They looked like beached whales in the gloom. Big and strong, but with the life knocked out of them. The death of an old man, not so old even. The dignity of a lifetime, crumbling into the air. Like a cat faltering in its steps from old age: so alone. My father is still trying to do what everyone expects to be able to do: move, talk, eat, breathe. Not so fast, Goldberg.

The shop I'd pinned my hopes on was still open. They only had brown pitta bread. But even this made my heart race in anticipation.

I buy him pills. Daddy goes upstairs and chokes and calls me. I don't hear him. So he comes downstairs, choking and half-naked, determined not to die up there alone. I suggest calling a doctor: he can hardly breathe. In between coughs he manages to blame the pills I got him.

I get the emergency number and the doctor's wife and then the doctor. Daddy calls me back. I hang up quickly and go to him. He tells me to call a doctor. I call the doctor again.

I comfort my father as he chokes. I say, 'Poor Daddy, poor Daddy.' I think of Lily's indignation when a pain won't go away – a rationality we have lost. I'm moved to touch him, I do care about this poor guy who's my father but seems all alone. I pat his shoulder. He pushes me away. I'm no help to him, we're both thinking.

'Hold your hand in benediction over me.'

Guy goes to the psychiatrist, jerking and twisting all over.
    Patient: Doctor, Doctor! You gotta help me!
    Doctor: Well, what seems to be the trouble?
    Patient (hands frantically flicking at himself): Oh, Doctor, I feel, I feel like, I feel like I got all these LITTLE GREEN MEN RUNNING ALL OVER ME!
    Doctor (recoiling with alarm): Well, don't brush 'em off on ME!

He might die at any time, I thought after the choking incident. I want to be here all the time, to be *with* him. On second thoughts, I don't want to be here at all. I leave him to his dying and drive back to London. He calls me up almost as soon as I get home: having heard that the roads were icy, he's been worrying about *me*.

MY VEGETABLE LOVE

Jumping may stop if Beans are kept cold
or dark for one month.

Jeremy began to take care of Lily most of the weekends when
I went to Oxford. I couldn't deal with her as well as my
father there. One day, when I was trying to arrange this, I
got a wrong number.

'Oh, is this 249 6254?' I asked, surprised.

'No, it's 249 6259,' said quite a friendly, low, male voice.

'Oh, I'm sorry. Close!'

'Well, I know this is the Age of Communication, but try
telling that to British Telecom.'

'The phones *are* lousy in this country. Yeah, I think I'll
blame it on British Telecom. Sorry to have disturbed you.'

'Not at all.'

We said good-bye and hung up. Then I thought about it.
Then I geared myself up – a process that took about half an
hour. Then I called 249 6259 again. I was too late. I got the
answering machine of a shop I'd seen once in Camden
Passage, that sold only old newspapers. I left a message:
'Hello, I called a minute ago, and you sounded a lot more
interesting than the person I was trying to get. I was
wondering if you'd like to meet for a drink. You can phone
me back on 249 8062. Uh, my name's Suzy.'

When sea-turtles meet up, they fuck for
hours, shell clacking against shell.

He held my neck in his hand. He held me as if I were a
motionless, feather-ruffled bird hunched chilly in his palm. I
lowered my head onto his shoulder, as his fingers moved up
between my legs. He seemed to know my stillness, to know
it sprang from passion – 'Love, and be silent.'

Later, I wanted to change the nature of the world, turn
anatomy inside out in order to consume him completely.

> 'Why have my sisters husbands, if they say
> They love you all? Happily, when I shall wed,
> That lord whose hand must take my plight shall carry
> Half my love with him, half my care and duty.'

I held octopus tentacles to his mouth and he ate them. I
offered him the oily blossom of an artichoke, and he put
pepper on my strawberries.

The house was full of azaleas and freesias.

> DON'T find a place in your garden for any plant
> because it has a neat habit of growth, or because it
> bears a showy flower.

'We fit together like two wandering continents,' he told
me, fitting us together.

Some men are so delicate (intentionally so). He was strong
and tough and patient and passionate. He was also married,
but having been married myself, I approved of adultery. My
friends dubbed him Mr Wednesday, though his visits were
much less predictable than that. He whipped me up into a
constant state of lust and longing, punctuated (with commas,

and exclamation points) by his presence. He was good at Erotic Torment: I retained my solitude, and was often too drunk to pick up the phone when he did manage to take his dog for a walk. But my fears of rejection fed my passion.

We never mentioned love. What use have birds and bears for words? He brought me champagne, a selection of old newspapers, and adornments in cerulean blue. I made him tiny naked female figures, suffering from surfeits of passion, out of fibrous clay that didn't need to be fired, that could be passed on to him without delay.

Looking at the spread I've laid out on the table, I begin to feel wary of the competition. I go back to the bathroom and dab on more perfume and inspect my face for spots with increasing dismay.

But later I'm reassured by the thought of the bite-size filo-pastry pouches filled with camembert and cranberries, the spinach and salmon mousse, the tomato I found almost ready to burst that now reclines, in slices, on a bed of fresh marjoram lapped by raspberry vinegar, the apple tarts with slices spread open like legs and the champagne, all left hardly touched as we fuck, bare and forked, on the floor.

He cups my cunt in his hand like a bread-roll, nudges the halves apart, and fills me.

Hull, pod, shell, bone, fillet.

He wanted the whole of me: there was some romance in junk after all. In orgies of counselling, so thorough it felt almost like I'd talked to a woman, he talked me until I was all talked out, and I'd sink contentedly to the only remaining task in life, to wrap myself around him until he left no room in me for thought.

124

THE STERNUM WAS APPROXIMATED WITH FOUR INTERRUPTED MERSILENE SUTURES. THE REMAINDER OF THE CLOSURE WAS DONE IN THE USUAL FASHION. THE SKIN WAS CLOSED WITH A 5-O SUBCUTICULAR CATGUT AND A CONTINUOUS PARALLEL MATTRESS DERMALON SUTURE. THE CHILD TOLERATED THE PROCEDURE WELL AND LEFT THE OPERATING ROOM IN GOOD CONDITION. SPONGE COUNT WAS REPORTED CORRECT.

NOT SO FAST

Dear Frances and Susan,
We are all working on finding a
solution to present worries, and your
whole-hearted participation is also
needed if we are to win. The stakes
are undoubtedly against us.
   When you were both little girls
your mother and father looked after
you. Now your dad needs just such
devotion from you.
      We're all counting on you.
            Uncle Samuel

Saskia is always telling me about all the things she's done, all
the New York doctors she's talked to in order to try to find a
cure for Daddy's incurable illness, and she's always badgering
me to do the same. Everybody wants me here to absolve
their conscience – and they go about it by plaguing mine.
They can't understand why I've not moved to Oxford so I
can have a ringside seat for this death, day in and day out.
Though not even Saskia can take that. Instead, she hires
housekeepers so that she can go to London in search of
miracle drugs.

   It's the old Cézanne's-wife syndrome: 'What was she doing
farting off to Paris to buy clothes when she could have been

posing for the great man all the time?' What was she supposed to do, sit around in rags in Aix, waiting to be painted by a guy who couldn't bear to touch her? Her every move is seen only in terms of how it affected Cézanne's life, when in fact it was the legitimate result of her acting out her own. People are so quick to decide who to throw overboard.

In *The Archers* on the other hand, no one leaves the 'm' off 'whom'. Everyone treats each other with respect and understanding, as if they've all been listening on secret wirelesses to the last couple of episodes so as not to tread unwittingly on someone's sore spot. No one's bad day is allowed to last too long: the script writers can't hack it, the fact that human behavior is on the whole base, crass, tragic.

What my father's friends fail to notice is that he himself is loath to see me sacrifice my life for his death. This therefore has to be done with some delicacy. A warm puddle of guilt spreads before us all.

I watch as my father becomes a tiny but perceptible bit worse every week. We struggle to communicate with him – the things he wants to say seem more complicated than they used to be, as if he weren't willing to compromise on what are after all his last utterances. His speech is laced with puns and other flourishes, now out of place like flowers in gravel. Sometimes, after several attempts to understand him, my only reward is the realization that what he's just said is, 'Call this living?' or some such quip.

Comforting sturdy keys of this typewriter that used to be his.

Two guys working in a factory, constantly pushing heavy metal beams around, above their heads.

First guy says, 'Hey, Jakey, where ya been lately anyway?'

Jakey: 'Took a vacation.'

Pause to thrust beams around.

'Yeah, Jakey? Where'd ya go?'

'Africa.'

'Africa! Well, what'd ya do there?'

'Went on a safari.'

'Wow, how was it?'

'Got eaten by a lion.'

'What do you mean? Why, here you are. You're alive!'

'Call this living?'

Saskia complains to me of Daddy's independence – he won't let her baby him.

'My mother was like that too,' I say, just to get her to shut up for the three seconds I desperately need her to shut up for.

> . . . formed and assembled, to create a flower of astonishing beauty and realism. From the simplicity of the pristine *Rosa Alba* to the luxuriant fullness of the *Mme Pierre Oger* . . . these lovely sculptures provide a diversity – and a unity – a dazzling display of beauty and colour that will bloom forever in your home.

I try to avoid going to Oxford when Franny is there. She bustles around and then leaves, disappearing completely – once her phone was even cut off and John turned up in Oxford to meet her when she was in Wivenhoe. We tried to entertain him. I found him rather handsome.

Franny astonishes me when we do meet up. There's a weird cheeriness about her – she sings as she prepares Daddy's supper. While she spoke to him of far-fetched cures one day, I noticed his attention was diverted by the glob of salad dip on the end of her celery stalk, which was in danger of being catapulted on to his trousers when she made her next point.

She fills this dying household with her junk, her multifarious purchases, her personal effects, links with the outside world which I envy her. There are disposable razors, blusher, dental floss, tampax and moisturizing cream left in the bathroom. By her bed I find perfume, a half-drunk glass of wine, an Afro comb, and Vidal Sassoon Hair Mousse. She even uses a kind of paper-clip I've seen all my life but never realized was a paper-clip. She's part of the world. I blow my nose on a bit of toilet paper and borrow the comb.

SHELL CLACKING AGAINST SHELL

I take him, in the Saab he can no longer drive, to his acupuncture appointment. I come back for him early, and the acupuncturist invites me in to the tropically hot room where my father lies, his flagging flesh pierced with a few needles. I'm appalled by Daddy's Ethiopian-style emaciation. His body before me wavers between being familiar, and lost already.

We leave, now both speechless.

Under the white light of the kitchen, his hands move up and down my body, lingering on my breasts. As I cling to him, I remember the charms of his body; they are by now listed, Marvel-like, in my mind. The black curls on the back of his neck, the soft flesh of his shoulders and the hard thighs. His jaunty step, and the way he fucks, frowning, murmuring, frowning, yelling, and sometimes weeping. The thick fingers that have loved me, that are driving into me now.

I open my mouth to kiss the corner of his lips, his chin, the hard line of his jaw, and press myself against him. A child's request for juice comes from the next room. Disentangling ourselves, the fridge is opened and the juice duly poured. Seated in a relaxed pose on a chaise-longue is a little girl with four dimples on each hand, watching a TV program that's as incomprehensible to me at that moment as it is to her.

'Don't you sit around feeling your balls all day?' I asked him one day, feeling his balls.

'Not when I have a heavy schedule.'

'There's nothing like it!'

'There's nothing like a lot of things,' he said, with his hand in my cunt.

'I want to fuck you till your ears drop off.'

I knew I was in a bad way when I could no longer read a book. I couldn't even get through the first sentence of a book. Never since my first painful exposure to Aesop had I been without the burden of a book.

The only things I could now read were personal ads, TV guides, problem pages, recipes, technical handbooks, and junk mail (I even stole Jeremy's sometimes). My life proceeded roughly along these lines:

> Do you know someone who would like the same peace of mind that you already enjoy as an AA member?

> You can buy swimwear especially made for women who have lost a breast, but lots of ordinary swimsuits will fit you perfectly well. You can make a good breast form for swimming by trimming an ordinary synthetic sponge to the shape of the cup in your swimsuit and sewing it in. When you get out of the water, press your arm against the cup to squeeze out most of the water.

> Wine is for drinking – not just academic study.

> For this experiment you will need a spring balance and some rubber suckers.

ENRICHED FLOUR (FLOUR NIACIN, IRON, THIAMINE MONONITRATE, RIBOFLAVIN), DARK BROWN SUGAR, PARTIALLY HYDROGENATED VEGETABLE SHORTENING, SUGAR, DRIED DATES, WALNUTS WITH BHA ADDED TO PROTECT FLAVOR, SALT, SODIUM BICARBONATE, SODIUM ALUMINUM PHOSPHATE, NATURAL FLAVOR.

It was after watching a weepy made-for-TV movie about a child dying of leukemia that I finally knew how sad I was about my father. That he was wasting away, that he was being taken from me, out from under me.

I had tried rationality: everybody has to go.

I'd tried: what good's life anyway – *I* want to die.

I'd tried viewing death as an injustice, an immense wrong done to every living thing. Apples falling off trees.

I'd tried general unfocused anger. I'd built a wall of it around myself, seeing everybody and everything – even spaghetti bolognese – in a ghastly new light.

I'd felt disgust, shame, indifference towards my father, and recoiled from his condition. I was so cold. I was so cold.

I'd tried self-hatred – thereby giving myself the excuse to slouch away.

And all to hide this little hurt, this little pain that was now revealed, the pain of loving someone who's dying.

After all after all after all, he was someone I knew and loved, knew and loved, and he was dying.

Suicide was suddenly the opposite of my desire: I wanted the whole bloody world to live! Life isn't so bad – there are redwood trees surging straight up, there's Cornwall, there are lampshades made of straw wound sweetly round in circles, there are certain female arms by Picasso, there are men who fuck you tenderly in the dark, there are the perfect forms of cats, there are electric heaters available at a fair price, bel canto arias and the first few pages of *Dombey & Son*. What the hell, what's wrong with it?

Only death.

THE DULL, STALE, TIRED BED

Dear Professor Cruikshank,
 I am writing to find out if my supervisor is
right in thinking that I would not be eligible
for another extension in order to allow me to
finish my dissertation. I understood that
extensions are given on the grounds of illness
or compassionate circumstances. My father is
ill and I am compassionate.

It's like showing your cunt to a doctor, having to tell strangers your father is dying. You feel so grateful if they're kind about it, since you're showing them something much more important to you than to them. You feel so soft and pathetic.

I got no answer to this letter.

Shortbread has beneficial effects on the soul. The warm glow it gives is better than alcohol, and more readily available than sex. Only 90p for a box (cardboard) of the best brand. Doesn't always work though.

I wrote letters all day, while vaguely stewing about Mr Wednesday's trip to Devon with his wife. I was finding it increasingly painful, the fact that he was married. And his wife was not my only rival: when he joined three evening classes and bought himself a two-disc computer, I should have known it was over.

He took me to Belgium for a long weekend. The jet-foil moved us swiftly away from England, two adulterers with our multi-colored consciences, and my fancy nightwear – I contentedly experiencing a jet-foil for the first time, and he clutching our return ticket. I followed him around boats and trains, longing to fuck him.

We took a room with long windows in a Brussels hotel which had once housed the Dukes of Brabant, and tumbled around on the bed at last, saying things like 'I'm hot for you.' We later ate crustaceans.

He called home the next day and found out his wife was pregnant. Their first child (she was by now only willing to copulate on ovulation days). Also, the cat had been poisoned. One or other. I didn't quite believe any of it, but couldn't say so. We stayed on another night – he was anxious to get back, but it would have looked too suspicious for him to return from his Business Trip early. In Bruges, he bought a smoked eel, a decorative biscuit in the shape of a cat, and some Ardennes paté to take home.

> Things that love nights
> Love not such nights as these.

That night, hankering to be home, he lay on the hotel bed and meditated out loud on the unpleasantness of my face upside-down. He bit me quite a bit. His caresses turned into condescending pats, mid-stroke. I kept feeling my breasts bulging out from under him in unexpected ways. He commented on how cold my skin felt. He became pedantic or admonitory on all subjects of discussion.

The next day, we pursued a good time with what time was left, except that every time he mentioned his wife, I cried.

All time tables are subject to alteration or cancel-
lation without notice. Connections are not
guaranteed.

It's the optimistic names of boats that make you feel sick
when they sink: the *Steadfast II*, the *Spirit of Free Enterprise*,
Q.E. III, *Perfection Personified IV*. We parted amicably
enough at Victoria Station and took our respective tubes
home with our respective duty-frees. I ate half a loaf of bread
and slept for fifteen hours – as per usual, I had not returned to
England refreshed.

Finally, clean the biting surfaces of your teeth.
Hold the brush so the filaments are flat onto the
teeth and use the vibratory brushing actions to
remove any food particles from the grooves and
crevices.

When they no longer vibrated like plucked strings in each
other's presence, they met up for a bad movie at the Screen
on the Green. After it he told her he didn't want to Jeopardize
his Marriage. Suzy was sweet and understanding, and as he
watched her walk down Upper Street, for a worrying
moment he thought, 'Why did I do that?' But he was
surprised later how she'd slipped his mind: in fact it was a
great relief. He returned home to his pregnant wife and
recuperating cat.
    Suzy returned home to a scene of devastation: Lily's toys
lay sprawled about the dining-room, as if a massacre had
taken place. One doll lay with her head to the side, legs
slightly open, smiling in death. Even the corkscrew lying on
the kitchen counter with its arms up looked dead to her.

'The grave's a fine and private place.'

MARZIPAN FRUITS

Franny and John had decided to get married, which pleased Daddy, who wanted to see us all settled. He wanted *me* to get divorced (Americans can't understand why this should take five years).

John wanted a Buddhist wedding: he'd been chanting his desires to the universe for many years. Franny was full of the joys of Spring. It did seem to be Spring. The necessity of flimsy attire, the Butlin's feeling of mob merriment, the pressure on everyone to change all previous plans – how I hate English sunny days.

When I asked Daddy what he wanted for his birthday, he said, 'Another birthday.' Instead, I bought him a few books, though I felt it was a bit presumptuous to choose him a book, when he'd been guiding *me* towards books all my life. One goes on needing a book right up to death – it's almost inevitable that every keen reader in the world will die in the middle of one, pages left unturned. On Daddy's suggestion, I had begun *Dombey & Son*, but hadn't gotten very far with it.

I made him a huge marbled chocolate and vanilla angel-food cake – like a foretaste of heaven – which Lily decorated with Marzipan fruit which he had always loved but could no longer chew, colored candy dots, and sixty-nine candles.

Franny's book on artistic abuse of materials was something of a best-seller, as art books go. She didn't bother to give me a copy, but I took a look at Daddy's:

"'I'm for an art covered with bandages,
I am for art that limps and rolls and runs
and jumps. I am for an art that takes its
form from the lines of life, that twists
and extends impossibly and accumulates
and spits and drips, and is sweet and
stupid as life itself.'"

The faculty of art to immortalize its creator has thus been eroded to the point where the impermanence of animal life is self-destructively emulated by the work of art.'

I was spending a lot of evenings driving around Chelsea, where it was easy to drive slow and look into lighted uncurtained windows. I was fascinated by all the different bijou decisions about decor, the disastrous lighting arrangements. But I hated to catch a glimpse of the inhabitants – I wasn't sure if this was because I was scared of being taken for a voyeur, or simply because I hated people. I liked to stop at the Midnight Shop in Knightsbridge on the way home, to get provisions.

There is so much love in your heart, you could
heal the entire planet.

Daddy asks me what I think of a Healing Tape some friend of Saskia's sent him from California:

Allow the love from your own heart to flow through
your veins, arteries, and capillaries, so that all your
cells are joyful as they go about their business of
keeping you healthy.
Diseases are the body's way of telling us we are on
the wrong track: every illness contains a lesson for
us to learn.

But when we are ready to make positive changes in our lives, we automatically attract what we need to help us in that task. The very fact that you have found me and this tape proves that you have begun the process of healing yourself.
Thanks for listening – I'll wait for you on the other side of the tape.

My opinion is that there are probably a lot of people waiting for that woman on the other side of eternity. But I don't say this to Daddy – Saskia might scold me for thwarting a potential cure. I avoid saying anything about it. I can't even look at Daddy any more without care over my expression. I go hard and blasé so he won't catch a whiff of my despair. So I won't too.

THE OLDEST HATH BORNE MOST

I saw him get horribly, repulsively, frighteningly ill, but still I didn't know he was dying. I knew he had a fatal disease, I knew his doctors had said he had little time to live, but I didn't realize he was dying. For months I watched his friends trail through Oxford to say goodbye, but I didn't say goodbye. They wrote him letters, but I didn't. They knew but I didn't.

On the morning before he died, my father was cold and gray, his lips turned blue, he could hardly breathe, he was barely conscious: I thought he might feel better after a sleep.

Franny and I stayed in the hospital that night, sleeping together in a little room for the first time in years. We were called back to Daddy's bedside at 3.00 in the morning. He was dying and I told him I loved him. I thanked him for enabling me to have Lily. Franny told me to shut up, but I went on. He revived enough to take my face once more in his hand. I revived enough to finally try to fight his death. I held his dying body in my arms, I tried to pump his lungs to make him breathe. I said, 'Daddy, Daddy, Daddy – breathe!' The doctor shook his head: nothing more to be done. 'Thank you for everything you've done for me, Daddy. Daddy. Daddy.' I held my father in my arms, for the first time in years, for the last time, my dear father who was still warm, still hot from life, and urged him to fight like an American, and he died. He died.

NOTHING WILL COME OF NOTHING: SPEAK AGAIN

'I DON'T WANT ANYBODY TO SEE MY FATHER, ESPECIALLY MEMBERS OF MY FAMILY, UNTIL YOU GET HIM OUT OF THOSE FUCKING RUFFLES AND THAT FUCKING PURPLE CURTAIN AND THAT FUCKING VEIL!' I yelled at the night porter, while he tried, and failed, to keep from smirking. I'd just brought Saskia straight from Heathrow to see my father. He was wheeled into a tiny chapel for us, an annex of the hospital morgue, where he'd been dressed in a white cotton sac, adorned with baptismal frills at the neck. We stood in the fridge with him for some time.

Later that night I returned to London to collect Lily. I was tired of being ineptly comforted by kind people who didn't want to touch me. When I got into bed with her, Lily seemed to know what was required and hugged me tight.

The betrayal of letting him die is matched by the sense of sacrilege when I tell myself that he is dead. I'm fiercely angry. I sit on the floors of loos and plot obscene punishments for everyone involved. I go over the house, where Daddy so recently was, again and again, and steal things. I wear his sweater, his coat, I take his money and some books and a cuff-link box I've always liked (that perhaps I even gave him), as if he hadn't given me enough. I take them as a posthumous show of love and try to forget what he hated about me. The Ph.D. that never saw the light of day, the light in Daddy's eyes. I grew up thinking that Art History was the only profession worth pursuing, that everybody's house is full of chaises-longues. What to do? What to do with the chaises-longues?

I want to murder his doctor. People tell me this is just a product of grieving, but I really *do* want to murder his doctor.

> *Dear Dr,*
> *I am writing to you on behalf*
> *of my family to thank you for all*
> *you did for my father, and to*
> *express to you our sincere wish that*
> *you take your N.H.S. 'courtesy*
> *calls' and your 'two sides to*
> *every issue' and stuff them up your*
> *two-faced medicinal ass.*

Franny is angry at me. She's full of the mysteries of death and doesn't want them disturbed by my anger.

CHRISTMAS MOURNING

Oxford

We all get together for Christmas six months after Daddy's death (as we must), Franny and I barely on speaking terms. The usual fury over the cooking, the gift wrapping and unwrapping, are all carried out under a cloud of mutual displeasure. I give her some nice ear-rings which she likes, and a star-fish pot-holder. She fails to give me a copy of her latest book, but offers instead a pair of naughty knickers that don't fit.

Later that afternoon, we watch *La Traviata* on TV together, and weep.

INDEX

Policeman, The French, 111.
Pollock, Jackson, *see* violence in art.
Post, *see* mail.
Post-coital productivity, 40.
Pouches, filo-pastry, containing such combinations as brie with blueberries, 124.
Poussin, Nicolas, 42, 45; *see also* Félibien.
Pulpits, Jack-in-the-.
Punch, Hawaiian, 5.
Pushchair, problems relating to, 79, 88, 90. *See also* stroller.

Racket, tennis, non-existence of, 35.
Rauschenberg, Robert, *see* violence in art.
Ready-mades, 35, 40; fake, 56.
Reagan, Ronald, only mention of, 26.
Rombauer, Irma, 5; complete recipe for French Pancakes, 484–5.
Rubens, Peter Paul, 16, 42, 45; *see also* Roger de Piles.

Sam, Uncle, the worried, 119, 126.
Saskia, 44, 45, 53, 55, 56, 57, 67, 126, 128, 138, 140, but not *passim*.
Sassoon, Vidal, 47, 129. (A.S.A.P.)
Schlamowitz, Andras, *passim*.
Schwitters, Kurt, *see* uses of junk.
Scum Gallery, 100, 103.
Shearer, Norma, wedding fiasco of, 116.
SINKIANG FAT-TAILED SHEEP.
Stroller, my adherence to, 4.
Sushi, the morally uplifting effects of, 105.
Sweets, *see* desserts.

Tenderness, fair imitation of, 87.
Thatcher, Margaret, the only mention of her, 26.

Thesis, *see* Pfro. Cuïrkchank.
Throwaway culture, *see* Lawrence Alloway. *Tip* dustmen.
Tickle-Two-Tums, 100.
Tinguely, Jean, *see* Kinetic art, next time it comes round.
Toasters, 3. If interested, *see also* bread.
Tomaatto, *say* tomato.
Torment, Erotic, if possible.
Truman, Harry, only mention of, 19.
Tyler, John, ditto.

UCCA forms, 70. *Try* not to think about it.
Ulysses, 27.
Upside-down, my face, 134.

Vermouth, *pronounce* ver*mouth*.
Vernissage, 72, 94.
Violence in art, 12–14, 65–66, 103, 137.

Wagner, Richard, inexplicable popularity of, 63.
Warhol, Andy, inexplicable popularity of, 96, 100.
Warholier-than-thou, *see* Campbell's Chicken Noodle Soup.
Washing-machine, *forget* it.
Wave, the New World's New, 96, 100, 105, 110.
Welch, Gene, the strange fortunes of, 22.

Yeats, William Butler, the stolen poems of, 27; 58.
Yoghurt, 28, 39, 56; Boysenberry, 93; Champagne Rhubarb, 28.